AFTER THE TRAIN

ALSO BY GLORIA WHELAN

Parade of Shadows

Summer of the War

The Turning

Listening for Lions

Burying the Sun

Chu Ju's House

The Impossible Journey

Fruitlands

Angel on the Square

Homeless Bird

Miranda's Last Stand

Indian School

THE ISLAND TRILOGY:

Once On This Island

Farewell to the Island

Return to the Island

AFTER
THE TRAIN

Gloria Whelan

HarperCollinsPublishers

Y
WHE

After the Train
Copyright © 2009 by Gloria Whelan
All rights reserved. Printed in the United States of America.
No part of this book may be used or reproduced in any manner whatsoever without
written permission except in the case of brief quotations embodied in critical articles
and reviews. For information address HarperCollins Children's Books, a division of
HarperCollins Publishers, 1350 Avenue of the Americas, New York, NY 10019.
www.harpercollinschildrens.com

Library of Congress Cataloging-in-Publication Data
Whelan, Gloria.
    After the train / Gloria Whelan. — 1st ed.
        p.   cm.
    Summary: Ten years after the end of the Second World War, the town of
Rolfen, West Germany, looks just as peaceful and beautiful as ever, until young
Peter Liebig discovers a secret about his past that leads him to question everything,
including the town's calm facade and his own sense of comfort and belonging.
    ISBN 978-0-06-029596-7 (trade bdg.) — ISBN 978-0-06-029597-4 (lib. bdg.)
    [1. Identity—Fiction.   2. Anti-Semitism—Fiction.   3. Jews—Germany—Fic-
tion.   4. Germany—History—1945-1955 —Fiction.]   I. Title.
PZ7.W5718Lo   2009   2008010185
[Fic]—dc22   CIP
                                                                                AC

Typography by Alison Klapthor
1   2   3   4   5   6   7   8   9   10
❖
First Edition

for Doris Vidaver

Every human being has his own gate. We must never make the mistake of wanting to enter the orchard by any gate but our own. To do this is dangerous for the one who enters and also for those who are already there.

—Elie Wiesel, *Night*

ONE

THE LAST DAY of school is a hundred thousand hours long. It's as long as waiting in the dentist's office or listening to your parents talk about what it was like when they were kids. The sun leaks through the windows, paints everything gold, and makes me warm and sleepy. Herr Schmidt drones on. I think about a soccer scrimmage after school and how I will be out with my rowing club on Saturday. I watch a fly, come to life with the warm weather, buzz against the window. I'm that trapped fly. I hear a train whistling in the distance and wish I were on it. I study the way Ruth Kassel's hair falls over her face as she leans down to write and the way she nibbles little slivers from her pencil when she is concentrating. She catches me staring at her and I quickly look away.

Herr Schmidt's classroom is the one I most dislike. Going to his class is like tearing off a scab. The war has been over for ten years. The Nazis are gone. It's 1955. Why should we have our noses rubbed in someone else's dirt just because we happen to be German? Our eighth grade is being scolded for something our parents did. It is something I don't want to hear or think about.

With his white-blond hair, pale skin, and long thin arms and fingers, Herr Schmidt looks like he lives in a cellar or a cave. He has an irritating way of drawing out his words so you are afraid he will never finish a sentence. "Ri-i-i-ight here in Rolfen," he said, "I am sor-r-r-ry to say there is the e-e-e-evil of anti-Semitism."

I'm tired of being told all the bad things about our country. Why can't he talk about the good things about Germany? I slump down and stare at my desk. It is at least a hundred years old. The carved initials in the desk are like ghosts of the students who have sat there before me. During the war the desk survived the bombs of the Americans and the English. I squirm in the hard wooden seat and catch Hans Adler's eye. His shrug tells me he is as bored and impatient as I am with the lecture.

As if it were just another lesson in grammar or arithmetic, Herr Schmidt prints on the blackboard the crimes of the German people and we copy them, each one like a scolding. *All over Germany Jewish converts to Christianity were expelled from the church.* When he speaks of what the church has done, Herr Schmidt looks serious and sad, as if to say, *People may do stupid and even evil things, but the church? How can that be?* But of course the church is not just a brick building that got up off its foundation and shook out the Jews; no, there was the pastor and those who chose him and paid him. When you speak of the church, you are not speaking of a building but of men and women. Even I know that.

We squirm in our seats. Hans speaks for everyone in the class when he wriggles his hand in the air and says, "We were just babies during the war. We didn't have anything to do with what happened to the Jews." I silently agree. Most people want to be good and they want people to believe they are good, so it's hard when you're made to feel guilty for something you didn't do.

Herr Schmidt says, "I know I am reviewing what we have talked of before, but I want to be sure you understand. I tell you these things so that your generation will not repeat the mistakes of your parents and their parents."

Dieter Kroner has been drawing dirty pictures of Herr Schmidt. Now he leans across the aisle and whispers to me, "That's all Jewish propaganda." Even I know better than that. Men have stood up in court and admitted their parts in what happened. There are government records and terrible pictures of men more dead than alive in prisoners' striped suits. It is all true, but I don't want to hear about it.

At last Herr Schmidt gives us our assignment to do over the summer. We groan. When we leave today, we want to close the door on the school and not think about it. Herr Schmidt says, "In spite of the terrible things that happened during the war, there were Germans who risked their lives to oppose Hitler. I want you to find such a person and write that person's story."

We push our way out of the classroom and into the hallway, where there's a sour smell: part sweaty socks, part stale air. Students shove one another in the halls and on the stairs as if they can't wait to get the day over with and get outside. Even the teachers seem impatient. Our algebra teacher storms up and down the aisles of the schoolroom, crumpling our papers and rapping the boys on the head with his ruler.

At lunchtime we kick around a soccer ball, an old size four with most of the leather worn away. Hans gets into a fight with Kurt Niehl because Kurt won't own up to a foul, and I have to pull them apart, getting an elbow in my ribs for my trouble. I make a nice shoelace pass, the ball rising into the air in a beautiful arc, lofting right over Hans's head and falling at Kurt's feet, but just at that moment the bell rings and we have to go back inside.

As usual Hans has done no homework and is unprepared for our Latin class with Frau Lerche. No one is more goodhearted or can turn on more charm than Hans, so most of the teachers forgive him his lack of interest in his studies, especially the women teachers; but Frau Lerche is immune to Hans's charm. Although he bats his long lashes at her and gives her his most radiant smile, she's not moved. When he translates *fastigium*, "height," as *fastidium*, "disgust," he gives Frau Lerche an opportunity for exercising her considerable sarcasm. "I have reached the height of my disgust with your translations, Herr Adler," she says, which makes Hans turn beet red. While Frau Lerche launches into a discussion of the beauty of the ablative case, I sit and stare out the window as if it were a postcard from someplace I'll never visit.

Finally the last day of school is over. Kurt and Hans and I run out of school, cheering at the top of our lungs. Hans says, "Herr Schmidt is so depressing. My father didn't have anything to do with what Herr Schmidt was talking about. He was in charge of supplies for the army."

Kurt says, "Neither did my father. He worked in a commissary, cutting up meat for the officers."

I don't say anything, because I've never asked my father what he did in the war and he has never said. I decide to ask when I see him in a little while. I've promised to meet him at the church where he works, but before I take off, I make plans for the evening with Hans and Kurt.

Hans says, "Let's go fishing on the river." He means the Wakenitz River. There is nothing Hans likes so much as doing something he's not supposed to.

We have been forbidden to fish there because the river is the border between us and East Germany. After World War II, the Allies split Germany in two. Our half of Germany, the West, is the Federal Republic of Germany. Across the border, East Germany, the so-called German Democratic Republic, is really controlled by the Soviet Union. The joke is that East Germany is neither democratic nor a republic. When Russia took over that part of Germany after the war, millions of Germans fled Communist rule. The refugees came looking for jobs and freedom, and our town of Rolfen took them in like abandoned kittens. Now the East forbids its citizens to leave the country, and those who do risk their lives.

Kurt says, "It's too dangerous to fish there since they've built the guard tower."

We watched the tower go up and the East German soldiers plow land at the border to make an empty strip where they can spot anyone trying to escape. Kurt's right—it's dangerous. But the big river here in Rolfen is polluted with sewage and with the ballast from the freighters. When we fish the little Wakenitz, we're careful to stay on our side of the river.

Kurt doesn't like going near the border. He and his family are refugees who escaped from East Germany and the Communists. He remembers what life was like under the Communists. Years ago you could cross the border; now, if you try to escape, the Communist guards shoot you.

Most of the people in Rolfen welcomed the thousands of refugees from Communist East Germany, but there are some in our town who resent the *Zugereisten*, the new people in town, because they take jobs and living quarters and food, all of which are scarce since the war. Bullies at school call out to refugees, "Get out of here! Go back to the pigsty of a country where you belong!" I have been with Kurt when the taunts are directed at him, and I have seen him grit this teeth and double up his fists, but he keeps his temper. Such taunts come from Gerhart Miller and Dieter Kroner and their fellow hoodlums, who are older and stronger than Kurt and me. People like Gerhart have to have someone to stomp on to make them feel superior. It reminds me of Herr Schmidt's description of what happened to the Jews.

Hans says, "We'll fish in that bend with all the alder bushes and willows. They'll never see us from the guard tower."

Kurt gives in. Kurt's always trying to keep Hans out of trouble, which is nearly impossible, and Hans is always trying to persuade Kurt to take a risk, which is also nearly impossible.

We plan to meet right after our supper. Outside school it's a different world. When June comes to our northern city, with its dark, chilling winters, it's like waking up to find yourself in a new country you can't wait to explore. We have the North Sea on one side and the Baltic Sea on the other. All winter long the icy wind grabs Rolfen between its sharp teeth and shakes and gnaws it like a dog with a bone. A chill like an evil spell lingers in the school. Though the war has been over for years, heating fuel is still scarce. All winter we have to keep our jackets on in school. Our handwriting looks like bird scratches because we have to hold our pens with gloved fingers. Now my jacket and gloves are shut up in the closet, and without them I feel so light, I could float right up into the sky. I'm sure that my thirteenth summer is going to be the best summer of my life.

TWO

AFTER SCHOOL I've taken to stopping at the redbrick church of St. Mary's, where Father is employed as an architect. Before the war he had been known for the churches he designed and built. In 1948, three years after the war's end, when I was only six, Father was hired by the city of Rolfen to help rebuild St. Mary's Church. We left our home in Swabia and traveled across Germany to the northern town of Rolfen. As I grew older and thought about the move, it seemed strange to me that Father and Mother traveled so far when there are hundreds of churches to rebuild in southern Germany, where we had lived. Once I pointed that out to Father, but he only said, "St. Mary's is a very famous church, and it's a privilege to help in its rebuilding." Today Father has promised to let me climb to the top of one of the steeples with him, the one that is nearly finished.

St. Mary's Evangelical Lutheran Church was built seven hundred years ago. Much of the church was destroyed by the bombing during the war, but when all the rebuilding is finished, the church's twin steeples will once again reach 125 meters into the sky. People who have lived in the town all their lives have been acting as if the vacant space left by the two tumbled steeples is as real as the steeples themselves were. In their stubbornness, they have been refusing to admit that the steeples were no longer there. When first I learned to find my way around the city, the directions I was given always used St. Mary's Church as the starting point. "It's two blocks over from St. Mary's," people would say, or "It's just around the corner from St. Mary's"—as if the absent steeples were still there to point the way.

In southern Germany, where we had come from, the churches were filled with statues and every kind of religious painting, but here in Rolfen St. Mary's is nearly bare, leaving you to imagine your own picture of God. When the church is filled with organ music and with the singing of the choir, it's like a cool drink of water when you're thirsty. Mother and Father attend services at St. Mary's every Sunday. Usually I go along with them.

There are Sundays when I want to sleep in, my

feather bed a downy nest of softness and warmth. I have a dream I don't want to let go of or a thought I want to chase. My bed is a safe boat on a great sea. To climb out of it is a risk I don't want to take. I want nothing to do with the business of washing and putting on my starched shirt, whose collar bites at my neck. I don't want to listen to Pastor Heuer warn us against the evils of the world. To him that means dancing and movies.

I make excuses, complaining of a sore throat or a headache. Mother becomes cross and insists I must get ready for church, but Father shakes his head and says, "It won't hurt him to miss church once in a while." Mother gets angry and there's an argument. It's the only time I see them quarrel with each other. It seems odd to me that in the matter of whether or not I go to church Father lets me do as I wish, when he's strict about everything else.

When I get to St. Mary's, I look into the small room where the church's great bells lie. When the church was bombed by the English and Americans on Palm Sunday, 1942, the bells fell to the ground and have remained there, lying on their sides like wounded soldiers. There was an argument in the town after the war. Some said the new bells should be cast from the old, that the new bells should have some of the old bells in them; but others said the injured bells were a reminder and must remain. "A reminder of what?" I asked Father, but he only said, "For everyone the memories are different, but for all they are sad. Nearby in Hamburg more than fifty churches were destroyed by bombs, and thousands of people in that city and here in Rolfen were killed. People can't bring back their loved ones, but they can rebuild their churches."

Today Father is eager to show me the progress they're making. "Peter," he says, "you can't know what comfort it gives me to see the church being restored. It's as if our country has been given a second chance. It's God's forgiveness."

From my visits to the church I have become friends with the workmen. "*Guten Abend*, Peter," they call out when they see me. They know I am the son of *der Meister*, the boss. They like Father, for he is often up on the scaffolding or down on his knees helping the workmen, as if he could not wait a moment longer for a brick to be laid or another stroke of the paintbrush, as if he were suffocating and knew he couldn't breathe again until the day the church is made whole.

While Father is the architect overseeing the rebuilding, he always says it is the workmen who are the important ones, and the workmen are quick to agree. Each one feels it is his special skill that is making the difference. Herr Brandt is working away at repairing the organ. "Young man," he tells me, "the organ is the soul of the church. Just think, when Johann Sebastian Bach, the greatest composer who ever lived, was a young man, it is said he walked a great distance just for the pleasure of playing the organ in St. Mary's Church."

Reiner Nordstrom, one of the stone workers, is repairing a stone carving of the Last Supper. "Look closely at the carving, Peter," he says. "See the little mouse gnawing away at the roots of the oak tree? The oak tree is the ancient symbol of Rolfen."

On our way up the scaffolding that covers the steeple like a wooden net, we pass David Schafer, who is inspecting some brickwork. Herr Schafer is a large, stocky man with a cap of black curling hair, sad eyes that turn down at the corners, and a watchful look, so that every time he sees you there is a moment before he relaxes into friendship. He is one of a handful of Jewish people who have come to live in Rolfen from East Germany. Today after the usual second of hesitation he greets us warmly. "*Wie geht's*, Peter? You have a fine day for your climb, but watch your footing." Then Herr Schafer says, "If you are very quiet, Peter, I'll show you something special."

Up, up we go on the scaffolding that hugs the church, Herr Schafer leading the way. I'm not exactly afraid of heights, but there's something about being high up in the air that makes you terrified you're going to fall and at the same time makes you want to take off into the air. As we near the bell tower, he pauses and, putting his finger on his lips for silence, points inside the tower where new bells will soon ring out. He is pointing to a nest and, on the nest, a large bird that stares at us as if daring us to trouble it. "A falcon," he whispers.

I whisper back, "She isn't bothered by all the work that's going on?"

"No, no. She puts up with us. She knows it is her territory and we are only intruders. Now I must get back to work. I'll leave the sky to the two of you. *Auf Wiedersehen.*"

The scaffolding continues up the part of the steeple already repaired. Each tile covers a section of the neighboring tile, so the steeple roof looks like the scales on a giant reptile's tail. I don't dare to look down. Each step feels as if I am putting my foot into air. At last we come to the place where the work has stopped. There the scaffolding has a platform where tile will be stacked, ready for the workmen. Father helps me to find my balance, and I settle down on the platform next to him.

Seeing Herr Schafer makes me think of the lecture we had in class. I ask Father, "Why would Jewish people want to live in Germany after what happened to them here?"

"You know the word *Heimat*," Papa says, "'home-land.' And you know the word *Heimweh*, 'homesick-ness.' You had it when we moved here from Swabia. You were lonesome for what was familiar to you. It is the same for Jews who grew up in Germany. There was a time when the Jewish people were at home and happy in Germany. Many have good memories of their childhood; it is hard to give that up. The language as well, Peter; it's a comfort when each word is familiar and will do just what you want it to. Jews hope things will be better now in Germany. The sad thing, Peter, is that when I hired Herr Schafer, I saw on his resume he had once taught philosophy at the university in Heidelberg."

"Why would a professor be laying bricks?" I ask.

Father says, "You know yourself that thousands, like your friend Kurt, have escaped to Rolfen from East Germany looking for a better life away from the Communists. Unfortunately there are no jobs here for professors. Schafer was lucky to get a job at all."

"But where did he learn to be such an expert brick-layer?"

"He's a resourceful man," Father says, in a voice he uses when he doesn't want to speak of something. He changes the subject. "You said you wanted a job this summer, Peter. Herr Schafer could use a helper. You wouldn't be laying the bricks—that's work for an expert—but you have a strong back and you could help in moving the bricks. What do you say?"

"Sure." I am excited at the idea of working on the church. I see myself getting up each morning and walking to work with my father. When the church is finished, I can say I had a part in it.

"I'll talk with Herr Schafer," Father said. "Now, what do you think of the view?"

Seen from atop the scaffolding, the town of Rolfen is like a picture in a book. There is the river and the canal that circles the town, turning the whole city into a moated castle. There is the gate, with its two round five-hundred-year-old towers. There is the main street, with its elegant merchant homes and the Shippers Society building topped by the golden sailboat, for Rolfen has been a trading port for a thousand years. There is the *Rathaus*, the town hall, which, like St. Mary's, was built seven hundred years ago and is as fine as any town hall in the world. And there is the school where Mother teaches kindergarten. This is Mother's fourth year of teaching, and when I walk down a street with her, it is never long before some little kid runs up to her and pulls at her sleeve and says, "Mrs. Liebig, Mrs. Liebig, remember me?" and she gives him a hug and he gives her a blissful look.

There are also the ruins where bombs fell and where

repairs have yet to be made; but today, as I look from up so high, they are hidden away.

Sitting in the clouds next to Father, just the two of us, I feel I have his whole attention. Away from everything, I have to ask the question that has been troubling me. I can't put Herr Schmidt's lecture out of my head. I know Father was in the German army. I wonder if he was part of the SA, the brownshirted shock troops, the men who sent millions of Jews to their death in brutal and cruel ways. I'm afraid to ask, afraid to learn the truth. He looks like the same father I have always known, neither short nor tall, with thinning blond hair streaked with gray. As usual the wire frames of his glasses have bits of tape where the frames bite into his ears. Under his suit he is wearing the tan wool cardigan that Mother knitted for him from wool she unraveled from an old sweater she found in a used clothing shop. I can't picture Father in a uniform. But I have to ask.

Right away I'm sorry. Father looks like I have struck him. "No, Peter. Never. I was a soldier in the German army like millions of other German men. As an architect I was ordered to construct barracks. I had nothing to do with what happened to the Jews. Did I guess what was going on? Yes. Did I try to stop it? No. It might have meant death for me, and I was a coward. Others took that chance, but I didn't. In that I am guilty." He is silent for a moment. I can see he longs to tell me something that will make me feel better about him, and at last he says, "There was one time when I had to make a hard choice and I made it. It's a thing that gives me great comfort."

I have to say, "Herr Schmidt told us we are all guilty because of what Germany did to the Jews. But I was only a little child. How can I be guilty?"

"Herr Schmidt should confine himself to scolding those who had a hand in the evil. He would find more than enough people to blame. There is no need for him to accuse children." He gave me a long look. "Most of all you, Peter."

"But Father, why did no one try to stop Hitler?"

"When a man is as powerful as Hitler was, it takes great courage to oppose him, but there were such men. In Swabia we lived not far from the home of Claus von Stauffenberg. Stauffenberg and some of his friends risked their lives to try to put an end to Hitler. But Peter, this is no place or time to think of such things. Let us keep silent on the subject."

So there was a time when Father had to make a choice, perhaps a choice of life or death for someone. He made the right choice, but a choice he doesn't want to talk about. Parents are mysteries you keep unraveling like the old sweater Mother took apart. Bit by bit, day by day, you discover more and more about them. I have taken my parents for granted, but Herr Schmidt's class is making me look at them in a new way, and now Father's insistence on silence makes me more curious than ever. I wonder what his secret is.

"Peter, only look around you," Father is saying. "We are on top of the world. How do you like it up here? It is easy to play God, *nicht*?"

It's true. Thinking of how little everything below us looks, I ask, "Father, do you think perhaps God so high up doesn't know about all of our small problems?"

"He is like the falcon with its sharp eye that misses nothing. Have you a problem for God, Peter?"

I shake my head no.

Father looks relieved. We sit there together, kings of all we see. "Father, if you were ruling the world, what would you change?"

"I'd make everyone's heart a little bigger, with a little more room for all. And you, Peter, what would you change?"

"I'd do away with all algebra tests."

Father laughs, and with one last look at the toy city beneath us, we climb down the scaffolding under the sharp eye of the falcon.

THREE

AFTER DINNER I get my fishing pole and hurry out of the house before my father can ask where I'm going and warn me against the Wakenitz. Hans and Kurt are waiting for me at the road that leads to the river. We do a lot of looking over our shoulders and sneaking down back roads. Every step toward the East German border is scary.

The last thing I want to talk about is school, but school is never far from Kurt's mind. He says, "I'm writing the essay for Herr Schmidt about Dietrich Bonhoeffer."

I should have known that Kurt would already have started his assignment.

Kurt, always happy to tell you how much he knows,

says, "Pastor Bonhoeffer was the head of a seminary not far from where we lived in East Germany. When a lot of the pastors in the German churches sided with Hitler, Bonhoeffer challenged the pastors to stand with the Jews against him. My father told me that Bonhoeffer said, 'The church is the church when it exists for every-one.' Hitler had Bonhoeffer put in jail and he was strangled to death."

Hans says, "Who wants to read that stuff when you're on vacation? Anyhow, what's the hurry? We've got the whole summer." I know Hans will still be working on his assignment the day school starts. I decide to get mine over with so it doesn't ruin my summer. I remember Father telling me of how in Swabia we lived not far from the home of Claus von Stauffenberg, who gave his life in an attempt to put an end to Hitler. I decide that's who I'll write about.

Because it's early in June and we're so far north, at seven in the evening it's as light as day out. We've turned off the road and are walking single file along a sandy trail that leads to the river. For a minute we stand solemnly in front of a sign with big red letters: ACHTUNG! BORDER THIRTY METERS. Kurt looks nervous. I guess he's thinking of his own family's cross-ing. He was little then, but he must still remember it.

Even though crossing over was legal then, they made it as difficult as they could for you.

A high fence topped with rolls of barbed wire stretches all along the border. In the distance the East German guard tower rises high up in the air like a church steeple. It's too far to make out the guard, but we're sure he's there, maybe even watching us through his binoculars.

"Do you think he can see us?" Kurt asks.

"Sure," Hans says, making a rude gesture in the direction of the tower.

"Stop it, Hans." I can't count all the times Hans has gotten us in trouble—not that we didn't help him out.

Kurt is still worried. "Do you suppose he's got a gun?"

"Of course," I say, "but he's not going to pay any attention to a few kids fishing on our side of the border."

We take off our shoes and socks and roll up our pant legs. As I ease into the freezing water, still cold from the melting snows of winter, I feel the sand squish up between my toes and the little pebbles dig at the soles of my feet. Even if the water is cold, this is the feel of summer. I tie a rubber worm to my leader and make a cast, careful not to snag my line in the overhanging trees and alder bushes. Hans plods downstream.

"Hey," Kurt yells at him. "You're stirring up the sand

and making the river cloudy. The fish won't bite." This is an old argument between them, and I pay no attention. I wander upstream from them, happy to be in the river with no classes to worry about for three long months. My job at St. Mary's doesn't start until next week.

I feel a tug on my line and pull in my first fish. It's a nice flounder. Since Kurt and I are forbidden to fish here, we can't take our catches home; but Hans's father, who manages the hotel, doesn't care, so we give the fish to the hotel and he pays us for them. I take a chance that the guard isn't watching where we cast and I try to whip my line across the wide river to the East German half, hoping to catch some Communist fish. I have to space my legs a little apart to keep from being pulled by the strong current that flows out to the sea.

Suddenly on the other side of the river I see a figure run across the bare strip of land where the guards have cut down the tall grasses so anyone trying to make it across the border will be seen. Amazingly, he is carrying a wooden ladder. I stand there frozen, watching him. He heaves the ladder against the fence, which must be five meters high, and throws his jacket over the barbed wire on the top. Then he hoists himself up, leaps over the fence, and falls to the ground. For a moment he just lies there and I'm sure he's dead, but no. He gets up and starts to run for the river. He's going to try to swim over to our side. I know I should do something, but I don't know what.

A siren goes off. It's so loud, it hurts my ears and nearly makes me lose my footing and fall into the water. Hans and Kurt have seen him. Hans yells, "*Schnell!* Quick!*" Kurt starts for the safety of the shore but turns around to watch the swimmer.

It's a young man, and now he's in the water and fighting the current. The siren is still sounding the alarm. Two soldiers are running in our direction. They stop at the river's edge and aim their rifles. I want to run away, but I can't move. He's halfway across into safe territory. Hans calls out, "Don't shoot! He's on our side!" And he is. Hans and I and a reluctant Kurt surround him. They can't shoot him without shooting us.

Reluctantly the guards put down their rifles. They shout curses at us, then walk slowly away, looking back a couple of times, as if the man might jump back into the river and give them another chance.

It's only now, while the man is shaking the water off him like a dog, that I feel a weakness in my knees and see that my hand holding the fishing pole is trembling. What was Hans thinking, calling out like that, and why didn't we have the sense to run away? Yet there the man is, although he's more our age than a grown man. He's escaped. They're not supposed to shoot someone on our side. If we hadn't been there, who knows what they would have done? I look more closely at the man. He's shaking with cold and fright. He can't be more than eighteen or nineteen. Kurt takes off his sweater and gives it to him. "Who are you?" Hans asks.

"My name is Gustav, Gustav Uhlich. My father was killed on the Russian front and my mother died when the Russians took over our part of Germany." His voice cracks and he gets a fierce look on his face. "I'd rather be dead than stay in East Germany under the Communists."

The three of us gather around Gustav as if he's a huge fish we have landed and don't know what to do with. He looks at us and gives us a big grin. "I was lucky," he says. "I owe my life to the three of you. If it weren't for you, right now my body would be floating away to the sea."

"What are you going to do?" I ask. I feel like we have some responsibility for our catch.

"I have to get dry clothes and then find a job. I was a baker's apprentice and I can bake as well as that baker. He was lazy and half the time he let me do his job. I can make *Spitzbuben*, *Vanillekipferl*, *Krapfen*, *Nussrolle*, *Obstkuchen*, *Apfeltorte mit Meringe*. . . . "

"Okay, okay, we get the idea," Hans says. "I'll talk to my father. Maybe we could use you in the hotel kitchen."

"That would be great. All I want to do is get my

hands on the proper ingredients. In East Germany there is no good white flour, no marzipan, no coconut, no dark chocolate. And margarine instead of butter. How can you be a baker?"

"Well, you won't find much of that stuff here, either. But at least you can complain about not having it without being arrested. You can come home with me, Gustav," Kurt says. "My folks and I came over from East Germany. We'll get you some clothes."

Suddenly Gustav sinks down and just sits there. His teeth are chattering. His smile is gone. It is as if he has suddenly realized what he has done. *"Ach!"* he says. "Those guys could have killed me! Did you see their rifles?"

The three of us march Gustav into town. We must look plenty funny, the three kids with our fishing poles and a wet Gustav. The Niehls listen with open mouths to our story and then run around getting Gustav clothes. They are so busy, they don't even think to scold us. Mr. Niehl is practically jumping for joy. Over and over he cries, "You put one over on them! And I'm going to rub their noses in it!" While Gustav explores the Niehls' kitchen, opening the icebox and the cupboards, Mr. Niehl is on the telephone to the town newspaper. In no time its editor, Herr Schultz himself, appears with his big black box camera to take pictures of a grinning

Gustav with Hans on one side and me and Kurt on the other.

I know I have to tell Mother and Father what has happened before they learn from the newspaper that I was fishing in the Wakenitz. They listen to my confession. At first they think I am making up the story, but I've brought Hans along to back me up. That is a mistake. "They pointed their rifles at us, Frau Liebig! They were going to shoot us!"

Mother sinks down on a chair, and Father goes pale and forgets to close his mouth. "Shut up, Hans," I say. "They were just after Gustav, honest."

"But we saved his life," Hans insists.

After Hans leaves, Mother and Father make me promise with my hand on the Bible that I will absolutely never go back to the river.

"Still," Father says, "to help save a life is a fine thing. Such a chance is not given to many people."

The amazing thing is there are tears in his eyes even though he has never set eyes on Gustav Uhlich. What is he thinking about? He reaches out for Mother's hand. I am sure it has to do with his secret. Mother must know what it is, and I mean to find out too.

FOUR

ALL DAY I WORK hard moving bricks at St. Mary's, but in the evenings I go out to play soccer or practice with my rowing club. The racing shell is light and slips through the water so easily, I feel as if it might take flight. I try to forget my troubles, thinking only of working the oars, pulling at the water and sending the boat forward, responding to the coxswain's urgings. Our little boat skims along the big river past freighters and barges that have sailed all over the world. I imagine myself on one of those freighters picking up a cargo of silk in China or stowing away and sneaking off a freighter in America and heading for the West and cowboy country. On Saturdays Hans and Kurt and I hitchhike to Travemünde, a resort on the Baltic Sea that has been there forever. Mammoth hotels rise like castles along the shore. The beach is dotted with rental chairs shaped like baskets, which we can't afford. Just off the beach is a park with a bandshell, and on the weekends there are concerts. The bandmaster is a jolly fellow with a fat belly and muttonchop whiskers who leads the band in rousing marches and corny waltzes while the old people keep time, humming along, and the little kids run around like unleashed puppies.

It is the sea that brings us here. The sea is always an escape, an escape from boring work and strict parents. I tell Hans and Kurt about the books I've read, Richard Henry Dana's *Two Years Before the Mast* and Joshua Slocum's *Sailing Alone Around the World*. We daydream about where we want to go. Kurt says he'd get a job on a freighter and sail to America, where he'd make a million dollars. Hans wants to go no farther than Sweden. "The most beautiful girls"—he sighs—"in the tiniest bathing suits." I dream about being a spy. I'd get into a small boat at midnight and secretly land somewhere in Russia to join a group of rebels plotting to fight the Communists. Then someone would make a movie about our secret adventure and I would star in it. The three of us sit on the beach daydreaming and letting the sun warm us until we have enough courage to run into the cold sea and splash about.

We don't go to Travemünde just for fun. There is

money to be made. The people who stay in the hotels are well-to-do; even those from Rolfen who come by train for the day are in a spending mood. If you keep your eyes open, there are little services you can do for the vacationers. Once settled in their basket chairs, they don't want to run across the sand to get a soda or some tanning lotion. The sand is hot and gets between their toes. Hans concentrates on the women, charming them with his big smile, while Kurt goes for the fat men who loosen their belts for comfort and don't want to tighten them again to get a coffee or sausage and roll. I look for mothers of little kids who are begging for ice cream. I get the ice creams and the mothers give me a tip. On good days we earn enough for third-class train fare back to Rolfen instead of having to hitchhike.

It is a Saturday in July when I notice a couple with two children, a boy of eight or nine and a girl a few years younger. The parents settle into their basket chairs and give pails and shovels to the children for castle building. The children run to the wet part of the beach, where the sand is good for packing. The girl starts her castle at once, but the boy heads for the sea, making dashes into the water, catching the waves as they roll in.

The basket chairs wrap around you on three sides. Seated in one, you can't see behind you or to your side.

Hans, Kurt, and I have funny stories to tell of things we overhear while standing unseen beside someone. While I wait with an eye on the boy and girl, who will surely soon be thinking of ice cream, I listen to an older man and woman who have no idea I am only inches away. The man has been swimming laps as if he were in a race, his arms mechanically rising from the water and cutting back into it so that he looks like a giant windup toy. As he hurries out of the water, he gives the boy and girl a long look. After rubbing himself briskly with a towel, the swimmer throws himself into his basket chair. I hear him say to the woman in the chair next to him, "Well, Gerda, so it starts all over again. I thought we were rid of them."

Gerda says, "You'd think, Konrad, they would know by now they weren't wanted here. First the East Germans come and take our jobs and make the town a slum with their sloppy ways, and now *they* are back."

I don't know who they are talking about; then it occurs to me that the couple with the two small children look Jewish. After all that has happened in Germany, how could the stupid Konrad and Gerda say such things? For the first time, I see why we need Herr Schmidt's class. I think of Herr Schafer and want to tell them to shut up.

Instead, just to show I'm not at all like Konrad and Gerda, I go over to the children of the Jewish couple and ask them if they'd like an ice-cream sandwich. They say an eager yes, and I buy each of them an ice cream with my own money. When they run to show their parents, the parents protest, calling me over and insisting on repaying me. When I refuse, they became suspicious of my motives. Why would a young boy who doesn't even know them bestow ice cream on their children? I can see they think I am in league with the ice-cream man and it's all some sort of scheme. I meant to be kind, and instead I merely look foolish. Reluctantly I take their money. I meant to do a good deed and this is what I get for it. I'm angry with them and with myself, for I understand that what I have done has smacked of condescension. As I look for someone to blame about the misunderstanding and not wanting it to be me, the thought goes through my head, *Jews are funny about money*. Disgusted, I see I am no better than Konrad and Gerda with their anti-Semitic talk.

Unhappy with myself, I turn away, thinking to plunge into the water and let the sea wash me clean, when I hear Hans calling to Kurt and me. I hurry across the beach, eager to get as far away as I can from the scene of my embarrassment.

Hans is hopping up and down with excitement. "I talked the man who rents the basket chairs and the boats into letting us have a sailboat for an hour," he says.

Kurt says, "We don't have any money to rent a sailboat."

Hans said, "We don't have to pay anything. We get the sailboat in exchange for the three of us staying late and cleaning up the beach and stacking the basket chairs."

"We'll be here until dark," Kurt says. "And it's hard getting a ride back home at night. Besides, none of us knows how to sail."

Hans says, "Peter reads all those books about sailing around the world."

"Those are books," I say, "and reading isn't sailing."

Hans brushes away my doubts. "You're always telling us that books are real to you."

I'm skeptical, but for weeks we have talked about what it would be like to be in a boat on the sea, and here is our chance. We drag the sailboat into the water. Hans holds it steady while Kurt and I climb in. Hans grins. "There's nothing to it. You just put up the sail and turn that lever at the back of the boat in the direction you want to go."

"What a fool you are, Hans," Kurt says. "That's a

rudder, and anyone can tell you that you have to turn the rudder in the opposite direction from the way you want to go." Kurt begins to describe some rule of physics, but I'm not listening. I'm trying to keep the boat from tipping as Hans climbs in.

Hans orders, "Peter, help me put up the long pole with the sail on it."

"That pole is the mast—and you don't put it up, you step it," I tell him. As soon as we have it in place, the wind seizes hold of the canvas and the sail begins whipping back and forth like it's a wild animal trying to escape. The boat tips one way and then another.

I shout, "Kurt, grab hold of the boom." Too late, the boom swings around and hits him in the chest, knocking the wind out of him. Hans pays no attention. He's busy letting out the sail, which immediately catches the wind. The sailboat is flying over the water. I hardly feel the boat beneath me, only the excitement of being carried across the waves toward the horizon by some strong force. The people on the beach grow smaller. The owner of the boat, looking like a cartoon character, is jumping up and down and waving his arms.

"What's he yelling?" Hans asks.

"He's signaling to take down the sail," I shout. "We're headed out to sea."

I can tell from the expression on Hans's face that the idea of heading out to sea is exactly what he wants. If there's a danger of drowning, all the more exciting. Desperately I grab at the sail and, fighting off Hans, begin to take it in. We rock wildly back and forth until at last the sail is down and the boat steadies. "How will we get back?" I ask, but the answer is there on the bottom of the boat. A pair of oars. Kurt is still groaning from the blow he received and refuses to have anything more to do with our adventure; and Hans is mad because I lowered the sail. He grumbles, "We could have made it all the way to Sweden."

"You belong to a rowing club," Kurt says to me. "Let's see how good you are." I row us back through the waves. By the time we reach the shore, my shoulders are aching. Rowing at sea is hard work. Kurt and I are so happy to be on dry land, we forget our anger with Hans until the owner of the boat and basket chair concession calls us *Dummköpfe* and a lot of other things, reminding us that we have to stay until dark to rake the sand and put the chairs away. "That means even if we're lucky and someone gives us a ride," I say, "it'll be midnight before we're home. My parents are going to be wild with worry."

Kurt says, "It was your idea, Hans. Peter and I should

go home and just let you clean up." But a minute later he is saying, "While we're raking the sand, we'll look for money. I'll bet people drop lots of coins during the day. Maybe we'll get enough to take the train back."

Hans is trying to talk us into using any money we find to rent the sailboat again, when we notice people leaving their basket chairs and hurrying toward the shore. They're looking out to the sea, where a small white figure is struggling in the water. The Jewish mother and father have waded out a way and are floundering in the waves, unable to swim and shouting for someone to rescue their son. The man I overheard talking about being "rid of them" plunges into the sea. His arms thrash in and out of the water, his head hardly coming up for a breath. The boy disappears beneath a wave. The next second we see him again. Another wave is coming, but the man reaches out, scooping up the boy. Tucking him under his arm, the man heads back to shore. The couple are crying with relief, thanking the man for saving their son. Even though the boy is now safe, the man who has rescued him keeps one arm around the boy as if, having saved his life, he had a stake in him.

All we rake up is a few pfennig, so just as I feared, it's midnight when I get home. To put off my scolding from Mother and Father, I tell them about the boy. "The man who rescued him looked like he didn't want to let go of the boy," I said. "Yet only a short time before, he was saying awful things about that family because they were Jews."

Mother says, "*Ach*, Peter, nothing is more precious to you than a life you have saved." Though she has never seen the boy, there are tears running down her cheeks.

FIVE

THE NEXT DAY I have one of my nightmares. The nightmares come less often than they used to when I was younger, but after Travemünde the bad dream comes slinking back like some animal living in the shadows. The nightmares began when I was little, hardly able to walk. In the dream everything looms over me. There are shouts. Someone is pleading. I am lifted up by a young woman; my face is wet with tears, my own and hers. I scream as I am pushed through a door or a window from darkness into light. I awaken, afraid my parents have heard me screaming, but at breakfast they say nothing.

Hearing my screams when I was little, Mother and Father would hurry into my room in their nightclothes, Mother's hair in a long plait, Father's hair standing up every which way. As I sobbed out the nightmare, Mother and Father would become as upset as I was, insisting that what I had dreamed was not true and that all was well. But there was something about the way they spoke that was not convincing. I saw they were troubled by my nightmares, and I began to believe there must be something real in them, something my parents knew and wouldn't tell me. The nightmares continued, but unwilling to upset Mother and Father, I managed to keep myself from crying out. Little by little the nightmares came less often.

After church I wander around the empty house, cursing the rain that is keeping me indoors and thinking of my nightmare and the secret I am sure my parents share. Father and Mother have gone to spend the afternoon with the Kesslers down the street. I begin poking about in Mother's dresser drawers. Mother is neat and organized and has a place for everything. She doesn't like me rummaging about. I am looking for the bundle of letters Father and Mother wrote to each other during the war. Once before, I gave them a quick glance, but it embarrassed me to see the soppy things they wrote, especially since they are so old, at least ten years older than the parents of my friends. Now I untie the ribbon that holds the letters together and begin to read.

In the early years of the war there are long sticky paragraphs about how they miss each other. Father is stationed in Berlin, and Mother worries about bombs falling on his office. She says the small garden she planted is producing vegetables and that there is little bombing in the part of Swabia where she is living. Soon she is writing about her work with the German Red Cross, helping soldiers. The letters are carefully written and give little information about what she sees. I guess that letters to soldiers were censored by the Nazi government. It takes me an hour to make my way from 1941 to 1944. I find no secrets and am hurrying through the last of the letters when something Mother writes puzzles me. The letter is dated July 30, 1944.

> *My darling,*
>
> *I have taken a great chance. If only you had been here to tell me what to do. Perhaps when you learn what it is I have done, you will be very unhappy, but I could not act otherwise. I believe it was a gift from God, who took pity on me because of my deepest longing. You will know what that is, but I can say no more.*

Mother is the most sensible person in the world. She thinks over everything twice and then once again. What chance did she take? And what is her "deepest longing"? Eagerly I open Father's reply.

Dearest Emma,

It is terrible that this war keeps us apart. I know your good sense and I cannot think you would do anything foolish.

He goes on to describe the weather and his life in Berlin and says he has a surprise for Mother. He has been given a few days' leave and will soon see her.

Quickly I turn to the next letter written after Father's leave. Mother speaks of how happy she was to see Father and how relieved she was that he had shared "the greatest joy and the greatest terror" she has ever known. After that some nonsense about picking wild raspberries in the fields and complaining that you cannot make jam without sugar. Father's final letter comes just before the war ends and is full of talk of a reunion and kisses to her and to "little Peter," and other such mush. There are no more letters, only an envelope with no address. I open it and draw out a picture of a young woman. I have seen the woman. She is the woman in my nightmare, the woman whose tears mingled with mine.

My hand shakes as I put the picture into the envelope

and carefully arrange the dresser drawer as I found it. I make my way into the kitchen and throw myself onto a chair. There in its usual place is the woodstove, which we use when there is wood and don't use when wood is scarce or too expensive. Also in its place is the nearly empty icebox, with its drip pan underneath that I forgot to empty, and the sink, which Mother scours so severely that the metal shows through the white enamel. At the window is the yellow striped curtain Mother made from an old dress of hers. On the floor is the oval rug braided with scraps of clothes; if you look closely, you can see Father's old tie and a blue shirt of mine that I have outgrown. Nothing has changed, yet everything has changed.

It is not a nightmare at all, but a memory. Who is the woman? What has she to do with me? Questions I have put out of my head now came tumbling out. I know about the birds and bees, so why haven't I wondered how Mother could have become pregnant when Father was away in the army for a year before I was born? Why, when there are so many pictures of me as a young boy, are there no pictures of me as a baby? Why has there been no mention of me in the letters until the last one? Why have we moved so far away from our home in Swabia? Why were Mother and Father so upset over my nightmares? What does Father mean by his talk of the one thing he is proud of? Little by little, like the colored bits of a kaleidoscope, all the questions form themselves into a pattern. Mother and Father are not my parents. Whoever my parents were, for some reason their identity is being kept from me.

The world shifts. I am no longer sure who I am. I have always been Peter Liebig—I even have my father's name—but now I could be anyone or no one. I look in the mirror that Mother keeps by the doorway so she can fuss with her hair and put on lipstick before she goes off to school each morning. A familiar face looks back at me, brown hair that flops over my forehead and always needs pushing back, brown eyes, the small white scar from my fall off Father's bicycle, which I had sneaked for a ride when I was seven. I feel if I pull the familiar face off like a mask, underneath I will see someone quite different, someone I don't know.

I wait to confront Mother. I will tell her I read the letters and saw the picture of the woman and I know the woman. Night after night the mysterious woman came to me in my nightmare wanting something. I will ask Mother, "Who is the woman? What does she want from me?"

Luckily another hour goes by before my parents

return, giving me time to come to my senses. How can I be sure the woman in the picture and the woman in my nightmare are the same? Even if they are, after all the years of caring for me, how can I confront Mother and accuse her of not being my mother? The whole thing might be my imagination. If I am wrong, how could I make up to Mother for such a terrible accusation? I will have to find the answers to my questions for myself. Though it will be nearly impossible, I will pretend nothing has happened.

Father goes off to his study to pore over his blueprints. Mother catches me staring at her and says, "Peter, why are you looking at me as if you didn't know me?"

I feel myself flush and manage to mumble, "You've got your hair in some new way. It looks very nice." It's a safe answer, for Mother is always looking for another way to wear her hair. "If I can't have new clothes," she says, "I can have a new hairdo, which costs nothing."

She glances in the mirror, the same mirror that has held my two images. "Why, Peter, imagine you noticing. What a nice compliment. For that I'll make you some cocoa. The Kesslers gave us a packet of chocolate."

"Not now, Mother, I promised Kurt I would meet him. We have to talk about an assignment from Herr Schmidt." I know that if I stay in the same room with her, I won't be able to keep from asking questions. I suddenly have to tell someone my story.

I throw on my jacket and I'm out the door, my mother watching me, a puzzled look on her face, for I have never been known to refuse anything with chocolate, which is my favorite and very scarce. I'm surprised and a little disappointed to find that the city takes no notice of how I have changed. People walk about under umbrellas. No one gives me a second glance.

I think about going to see Hans. Hans works for his father, who manages a hotel in town, and Hans is making what seems a small fortune by carrying travelers' luggage up and down stairs. "I smile a lot," Hans said. He gives Kurt and me a huge grin as a sample. "No matter who they are, I tell them the hotel is honored to have such important guests. I pretend to mistake the women for movie stars and the men for important politicians. I get huge tips." I think of telling Hans, but he says whatever comes into his head, and he would blurt out my story the first chance he gets. I decide to talk to Kurt.

Kurt is working in the market, where his father is a butcher. He tells Hans and me how he is instructing the owner of the market on better ways to run his business. The Niehl family lives in the upstairs of a small house near the Lindenplatz. Herr Niehl is a jolly man, and when I go with Mother into the meat market where he works, he always has a friendly greeting and a little joke. Kurt's mother is more reserved. Kurt says she misses her family in East Germany. Visiting back and forth isn't allowed.

I tell Kurt I want to see him for a few minutes outside. Gustav is in the kitchen, busy at the stove, a dish towel tucked in his belt. There is the smell of walnuts. He pulls a cake out of the oven. Since Gustav has moved in with the Niehls, the whole family has gotten fatter.

Frau Niehl says, "Gustav insisted on making a *Nusstorte*. You can take some home with you when you get back. Don't go far now. Dinner is nearly ready."

Kurt and I head for the path that runs along the river. A flock of migrating ducks drifts down onto the river without a splash. They are like messengers from some wild and distant place. I imagine being an explorer traveling to the Arctic or maybe the Antarctic.

Kurt says, "The ducks will be gone by morning. Someone will shoot them. You can't blame them. At the shop they have a terrible time trying to find meat to sell, and a roasted duck is plenty tasty."

He sighs. But I can't tell whether the sigh is for the fate of the birds or for a longing to taste one of the ducks. I want to tell Kurt what I have discovered, but now that I am with him I, can't bring myself to give away my secret. He will think I have taken leave of my senses. I clear my throat. "I just read this strange story," I say.

"What strange story?" Kurt asks.

"This boy found out he wasn't who he thought he was—that he was adopted."

"What do you mean? Are you making up one of your weird tales?"

It's true I like to make up weird tales. I made up a great story about inside-out creatures whose insides were all on the outside. It was really disgusting. Another one I invented was about how gravity doesn't work anymore and the whole world is littered with all the stuff that doesn't fall down but just floats around in the air.

"No, it's a real story," I say. "I read it in a book. The boy has nightmares about a woman. One day he sees some letters and a picture. When the boy sees the picture, he recognizes the woman from his nightmare. It's his *Geburtsmutter*, his birth mother. He realizes he's adopted."

"How could he be sure the woman in the picture was the same woman?"

"She doesn't just look the same, she feels the same."

"How come you know how he felt, and how come you came all the way here at dinnertime to tell me something you say you read somewhere?"

"I'm just saying what was in the story. He saw some letters that suggested that his parents weren't his real parents."

"So why doesn't he just ask his parents?"

"He doesn't want to upset them. Suppose he's wrong? It would be awful if he accuses them of not being his parents. They'll think he's out of his mind and probably never forgive him."

"He can look for his birth certificate," Kurt says.

"With the bombing during the war, a lot of stuff like that has been lost."

"I know. When we escaped from Gross Methling, in East Germany, we had to leave all our papers behind. Anyhow, why should you worry about some boy in a story?" Kurt gives me a suspicious look.

Quickly I say, "I don't know. It was just kind of interesting. I guess thousands of kids lost their parents during the war. That boy has new parents, and they're good parents, so it's no big deal."

Kurt says, "When you've got something besides stories from some crazy book, come and see me."

By now we're back at the Niehls' house. Frau Niehl wraps up three slices of *Nusstorte*, and I carry them home, eating only a small bite from each piece.

SIX

THE NEXT DAY at work my head is still dizzy from finding the woman's picture and trying to make sense of it. I can't get used to myself as someone else, someone I didn't know and don't know how to know. I think about asking my father, but I'll have to confess to reading the letters. Besides, I'm not sure I'm ready to hear what he says.

I want to escape the puzzle and decide to spend the evening doing my assignment. I head for the library with my notebook and ask the librarian, Frau Kaiser, if she can find me some information on Claus von Stauffenberg.

"Claus von Stauffenberg," she says. "A good man who came to an unhappy ending. Let me see what I can dig up for you." She bustles about and returns with a stack of old newspapers and magazines. "There are some tasty bits here," she says, and hands me the bundle as if it were a plate of delicious candies.

I turn over the papers, chew my eraser for a bit, and plunge in. I learned long ago that nothing is as scary as a blank page, so I fill it up with the first thing that comes to mind: my wish to find good people in Nazi Germany. Stauffenberg, I learn, was born to an ancient and aristocratic south German Catholic family. I do the arithmetic and figure out he would be forty-eight now. He grew up with his two brothers, Alexander and Berthold, in a sort of castle in Jettingen, a little town in Swabia. I look up the town on a map. Jettingen is only a short distance from the town of Ulm, where we lived when I was little and where Mother waited out the war. No wonder Father knew about Stauffenberg. He must have been a legend to everyone around there.

Stauffenberg was tall—six foot three—and handsome. He was brilliant in school, wrote poetry, and could speak fluent Greek and Latin. He read every book he could get his hands on, but he was no bookworm. He excelled at sports, was crazy about horses, and even rode with Germany's Olympic equestrian team. He was going to be a musician or an architect like my father, but he finally decided to follow the family tradition and become a soldier. Because of his love for horses he joined the cavalry.

During the war he fought with the German army: in the Sudetenland (the western part of Czechoslovakia), and in Poland, France, Russia, and Africa; but all the while he despised Hitler and especially the Nazi Party's paramilitary SA troops. *Kristallnacht* was a turning point for Stauffenberg. On that night the stores and homes of Jews were destroyed, their glass windows shattered. Jews were dragged out onto the streets and humiliated. Stauffenberg was horrified at what Hitler was doing to the Jews. His brother, Alexander, was married to a woman with Jewish grandparents, and Stauffenberg had many Jewish friends. As early as 1938 he was plotting against Hitler.

He thought that because they were serving under Hitler, he and his fellow soldiers were fighting and dying for a dishonorable cause. He said he was "hungry for honor." He believed that God had assigned him the mission of getting rid of Hitler, but it was no easy job. Hitler kept changing his headquarters, and giving out information on Hitler's whereabouts was punishable by death. Stauffenberg himself couldn't get close to Hitler. Impatient and frustrated, he asked friends of his who felt as he did, "Is there no officer in the Führer's headquarters capable of shooting that beast?"

In April of 1943 he was serving in North Africa with the Afrika Korps when his vehicle was strafed by British fighter-bombers. He lost his left eye, right hand, and two fingers of his left hand. After he recovered from his injuries, he was promoted and made staff officer to the commander of the reserve army. In his new position, he knew, he would at long last have a chance to be in the same room with Hitler. Stauffenberg decided the time had come. He said, "I'll kill him myself with my three fingers!"

On July 20 he flew to meet with Hitler at Wolf's Lair, one of Hitler's retreats. There were 80,000 land mines encircling Wolf's Lair to protect Hitler from anyone trying to steal into his headquarters. Hitler never imagined that it would be one of his own officers who would try to take his life. In his briefcase Stauffenberg had two bombs. Using specially made pliers because of his injured hand, he armed one of the bombs by breaking a capsule with acid in it. In less than half an hour the acid would eat its way into the fuse and set off the bomb. Once Stauffenberg broke the capsule, there was no going back. In the meeting room he placed his briefcase under the table just where Hitler would be sitting, explaining that because of his injuries in Africa, his hearing was bad and he wanted to be close to Hitler so he could hear all the Führer had to say.

Stauffenberg arranged for one of his coconspirators to summon him to the phone once the briefcase was in place. He left before Hitler entered the room. The plan was that as soon as he knew Hitler was dead, he would fly back to Berlin, take over the radio transmitters and police stations, and organize a coup against the Nazi government. He wanted to work out a conditional surrender with the Allies. He didn't want just to get rid of Hitler, he wanted to destroy the whole Nazi regime. When he was a short distance from the meeting room, he heard a huge explosion. A dead man was carried out on a stretcher with Hitler's coat over him. Stauffenberg was sure the dead man was Hitler.

At once Stauffenberg flew to Berlin and announced, "The swine is dead." He began to arrest the Nazi leadership, including his own superior, General Fromm.

Hitler wasn't dead. He had been protected from the blast by the heavy oak meeting table. Perhaps someone had also moved the briefcase. The man carried out under Hitler's coat was not Hitler. Hitler's uniform was in shreds and one eardrum had burst from the blast, but he was still very much alive and the war was still on. After surviving the explosion, Hitler bragged, "I am indestructible!"

Hitler vowed a terrible vengeance. He ordered the Stauffenberg family exterminated down to the last member. Stauffenberg was executed that very day. After he was buried, Hitler had his body dug up and burned, and the ashes scattered to the winds. More than five thousand people thought by Hitler to have some connection with Stauffenberg were arrested and tortured. More than two hundred were executed. Hitler insisted on watching some of the executions himself. Both Stauffenberg's wife and one of his brothers were sent to concentration camps. His other brother was strangled to death slowly. Almost all the Stauffenbergs' close relatives were imprisoned. The Stauffenbergs' five children were placed in foster homes and given new last names.

I read and reread every word, but I can't discover what happened to the children.

Pencil in midair, I stop reading. Some of Stauffenberg's children were just toddlers. Could I be one of those children? There is my nightmare and the picture of the mysterious woman. Hasn't Father mentioned Stauffenberg himself? Is he trying to tell me something? When Father refuses to make me go to the Protestant church on Sunday, is that because I am Catholic, like the Stauffenbergs? I love Mother and Father, but how proud I would be to find that I belong to the aristocratic

Stauffenberg family! How honored I would be to be related to that hero.

Hastily I finish my assignment and run into the library bathroom. For the second time I find myself staring into a mirror, wondering who I am. This time I'm trying to see if I resemble Stauffenberg. I am of medium height and Stauffenberg was six foot three; still, I am only thirteen and haven't reached my full height. I have to know the truth. I decide I can't wait another minute. I head for St. Mary's, where Father went after supper to meet with Pastor Heuer over some construction problem that has come up.

He looks pleased to see me. "One minute, Peter, and I'll be right with you." I shift from one foot to the other while Father and Pastor Heuer bend over the blueprints of the church and mumble about this and that. At last father follows me out of the church. It's nearly nine o'clock, but in the long June evenings the sun is still above the top of the row of old merchant houses. I like walking down the main street with my father. Lots of people know he is the architect working on St. Mary's. I love him and I'm proud of him, but guilty and ashamed as it makes me feel, I'd be prouder of being the son of Count von Stauffenberg.

Mother says you can see through me like a pane of

glass, and it must be true, for after giving me a brief look, Father says, "Peter, is something bothering you?"

I keep my head down, concentrating on kicking aside the maple tree seeds that have spiraled down onto the sidewalk. "Father, you know those nightmares I used to have, and I would cry out and wake you and Mother up and Mother would get so upset?"

"Yes, of course I remember. But you don't have those nightmares anymore. Why do you bring them up now?"

"I still have them, only not so often and I don't tell you because I'm not a baby anymore, and besides, I saw how much they worried Mother."

Father looks troubled. "You say you still have the nightmares?"

"Yes, but that's not what I want to talk about. I was rummaging around in Mother's dresser. I know I shouldn't have, but I thought there was something you and Mother hadn't told me, some secret. I saw your letters to Mother and hers to you." My voice gets hoarse and I feel my face grow red. "I saw what Mother said about taking a great chance and how maybe she shouldn't have. She worried that you wouldn't approve. There was a picture. The picture was of the same woman in my nightmare." I stop talking because Father's face is stormy.

Roughly grasping my arm, he pulls me toward an iron bench. "Sit down." He shoves me onto the bench and settles down beside me. "Peter, you had no right to go through your mother's things. It's inexcusable to read private letters."

"I guessed you had some secret, but you would never tell me what it was. Now I know I'm right."

Father puts his hands to his face, then quickly takes them away and glances about to see if anyone is watching. The street is deserted except for a large tabby cat prowling among the shrubbery, searching for a bird. "You're right, Peter. We have not told you the truth. Your mother was very much against it and I went along with her wishes. If you went to her as you came to me just now, bursting with your story of reading the letters and worst of all trying to connect the woman in the picture with the woman in your nightmares, I tell you honestly, Peter, it would break her heart. I promise I will talk with her, but give me a few days to think of how I will do it."

"Can't you tell me now? I won't tell her I know."

"No, Peter. Hard as it may be after what you have seen, you must trust me."

"Can I ask just one question, Father?"

"Just one, but then the subject is closed until I am

ready to discuss it with you."

"Am I related to Claus von Stauffenberg?"

"Stauffenberg! Whatever gave you that idea? Certainly not! Now, I have answered your question. Not another word on the subject."

Father appears shocked at my question, but I can't tell whether I am very wrong, which I refuse to believe, or whether I have hit upon a truth Father will not admit. Maybe he is afraid the Stauffenbergs will take me away. I promise not to say another word to him or to Mother, but I hatch a plan. I have no intention of waiting for days or weeks or years to find out who I am, and I didn't believe Father when he said I am not related to Stauffenberg. I am sure he is just trying to put me off.

After dinner I sneak some good writing paper from Father's desk and a picture from our photograph album of me taken on my fifth birthday holding a pet rabbit I had been given as a present. I have no address for the envelope, but surely everyone around the area of Jettingen will know the Stauffenberg family.

Dear Frau von Stauffenberg,
   I want to tell you how much I admire your husband. He is a great hero and you must be very proud of him. I am sorry to trouble you

and this might be a shock, but I could be a long-
lost member of your family. I know that your
children were taken from you and the children
of your husband's family were taken from them.
Although my parents won't tell me where I came
from, some things they have said make me
think I might be a Stauffenberg. I am a thirteen-
year-old boy who grew up near you and who
doesn't know who his real parents are, although
I have very nice parents now. I am sending you
a picture of me so that you or someone in your
family can recognize me. I would appreciate
hearing from you as soon as possible.

Peter Liebig (von Stauffenberg?)

I stuff the letter into an envelope and, before I lose courage, run to the mailbox and drop it in. It's nearly dark now, but I find Hans and Kurt under a streetlight. We walk along the darkened streets planning what we will do on the weekend. I feel bad, knowing that if I go and live with the Stauffenbergs, I might not see Hans and Kurt again. I tell myself that I will send them train tickets and comfort myself with thoughts of going to meet them at the station in a big black Mercedes—and maybe with a chauffeur driving.

SEVEN

I TOSS AND TURN all night. When morning finally comes, the bedding looks like a squirrel's nest or a dish of noodles. As I dress, I imagine the Stauffenbergs seeing my letter, recognizing me, being excited, and sending me the fare to come and join them. My summer will be spent in their castle getting to know my real family. When I finally come downstairs, I look at my mother and try to guess if Father has said anything to her about my discovery, but she looks just as she always has and warns me I'll be late if I don't hurry.

In the early morning as Father and I walk to the church together, the summer day is still cool. Mist covers the ground. As the sun warms the earth, the town gradually appears through the mist so that it looks as if it has been newly made. As we walk along, I keep hoping Father will say something about my nightmare and the woman, but he doesn't. Instead he uses the walk to work to tell me all his problems. Crucial construction material has not been delivered, and what has been delivered is not what was ordered. A workman is drinking on the job. Father is having an argument with the pastor of the church about how to place the pulpit. I guess that he is using a list of problems to evade what I really want him to talk about.

My job at St. Mary's is to fill a cart with bricks and wheel it over to where Herr Schafer or one of the other bricklayers is working. After all the months shut up in the classroom, I thank my lucky stars that I am outside in a world of trees and sky and sun with not a desk in sight.

For an adult Herr Schafer is easy to be with, and I feel as if he is someone I have known for a long time. He dresses like the other workers, in an old shirt and trousers, but he does not look like them. For one thing, he wears old-fashioned rimless glasses, and for another, though he is an excellent workman, he has always a look of not being where he is. I remember Father telling me that Herr Schafer was a professor, and it's not hard to imagine him at the head of a classroom. I think of

Herr Schmidt's lectures and wonder what happened to Herr Schafer, as a Jew, during the war.

While the other workers gather at noon for their lunch—sausages, big hunks of cheese, and cold bottles of beer—Herr Schafer sits by himself with his lunch and a book. The other workers like to joke, and I see that they are uncomfortable telling their earthy jokes with me nearby; so I take my own book and lunch to where Herr Schafer is. Sitting next to him is like having a book in your hands and not being able to look inside. At last I ask him, "How did you come to be a bricklayer?"

He doesn't answer my question but only says, "Nothing wrong with bricklaying. In his spare time the former British prime minister, Winston Churchill, was a bricklayer." In a more serious voice he adds, "There aren't many jobs and bricklaying is steady work. You have only to look around you at the buildings that have fallen apart from the bombs. All of Germany is like this, and the German people won't put up with such messes. There will be work for us bricklayers for years to come."

Still, I don't believe Herr Schafer will spend the rest of his life laying bricks. The books he reads are thick and have many pages. As he turns the pages, he underlines heavily and sometimes mutters angrily as if the book were a person who is arguing with him.

In his bricklaying Herr Schafer is a perfectionist, which means I have a hard time. I dream of making my own contribution to the building of the church by laying neat rows of bricks that will be there for centuries, but all he will let me do is to carry the bricks and stack them near the spot where he wants them. Sometimes he finds fault with my work. "Peter, you have only to breathe on that pile of bricks you made and they will fall over in a heap. You must build the stack so that the bricks on the outer walls lean in slightly." He is full of brickman's language, as much trouble to me as Latin is. I have to learn the meaning of *closure*, *wythe*, *header*, and *stretcher courses*. I discover that a "rowlock sailor" is a brick that stands upright with its broad side facing out while a "soldier" is a brick standing upright with its narrow side facing out, as if all sailors were fat and all soldiers were thin. It's my job to see that the bricks have just the right degree of moisture. After I stack them, I have to take one of the bricks and put drops of water on it. If I can still see the damp spot after a minute and a half goes by, all is well. If the damp spot disappears, I have to get pails of water and douse the bricks so they won't absorb the moisture from the mortar and weaken the joints between the bricks.

Herr Schafer is a pleasure to watch. With a long

sweep of his trowel he can throw a mortar line along the tops of six or seven bricks and lay each brick level and plumb. Father knows all about his skill. "The architect has only an idea, Peter," Father says. "His idea doesn't exist until the workman brings it to life."

Herr Schafer listens carefully to Father, but he doesn't always agree with him. When he doesn't, he says so. "Herr Schmidt, excuse me, but the pattern of bricks you're suggesting for the part of the east wall we are repairing will be like a dog with no ears and no tail. If you look at the old pictures of the church, you'll see there was a course of brick like so." He sets the bricks on the floor of the church to show what he means. "You see how that gives the wall a pretty line?"

"Yes, yes, Herr Schafer, I agree. By all means let's follow your suggestion."

But sometimes Herr Schafer and Father get into an argument. Then Herr Schafer grows very quiet and aloof. Father gets authoritative and plays the boss. Though Father fumes a little, in the end it's usually Father who gives in. Herr Schafer smiles again. Father laughs and teases him. "I suppose you'd go on strike like your thirteenth-century brethren."

When I ask Herr Schafer what Father means, he says, "Seven hundred years ago the masons in France who were laying the bricks and stones on French cathedrals were commanded by the bishops to cut their long hair and shave their beards. They refused and stopped working. The bishops gave in."

After one such argument, Father says, "You see how Herr Schafer can tell the boss what must be done? That's the thing about these Gothic cathedrals, Peter, that people don't always realize. These churches are the first great monuments built by workmen who were their own masters. Just think of the pyramids—the slaves who built them carted stones under the scourge of the Egyptian lash. Thousands of workmen died to build the pyramids. In the twelfth and thirteenth centuries, when the great Gothic churches were built, men built with their hearts and minds as well as their backs. It was no longer just the master who decided what must be done. No, the workmen had a say. All the skill and imagination of the workmen was added to that of the master, and look what beauty came of men working freely!"

"How did that happen, Father?" I ask. I like the idea of the workman having a say, for Herr Schafer is my boss and I'm his employee.

"The monks in those days came from wealthy families. In the monasteries the monks spent all their time in prayer and had servants to wait upon them just as they had in the homes where they were raised. Along came St. Benedict, who said his monks must do physical work as well as pray. 'Idleness is the enemy of the soul,' St. Benedict said. Suddenly labor was honorable and respected.

"There was something else. Everyone in the city or town where the church was going up felt a part of the building of the church. In the Middle Ages life was hard. The cathedral brought some beauty into people's lives. It was a promise of what was to come in God's kingdom. These churches have been called the Bible of the poor. People in those days could not read or write, and so the stories of the Bible were told in the sculptures and in the stained-glass windows." After a moment Father says to me, "And not just the New Testament, Peter, but the Old Testament as well."

On our walks to and from St. Mary's, Father has begun to tell me about the building of the churches, so our walks are like chapters in a book. "Life in the Middle Ages, Peter, was brutish. Babies died in their mothers' arms; there were famines and plagues that killed half the population of a town. In all that ugliness and misery the beauty of the church was a promise of what was to come in God's kingdom; the promise of Heaven enabled people to endure their cruel world."

With the steeples nearly finished, preparations are

being made for transporting the new bells to St. Mary's. "Bells have always been important," Father says. "In the Middle Ages they rang out to warn of storms that might threaten a harvest, and four nights of the year, when witches were said to be abroad, the bells sounded all night to keep them away."

Because I have something to do with all the changes to St. Mary's, I urge my parents to arrive at the service early on Sunday. I want to see the pleased looks on the faces of the parishioners as they examine the progress that has been made. Of course they haven't counted the bricks I have moved about, but I have counted them. I am proud of the church and sure that God is as well. I like to think of him up there, a Herr Schafer with a long beard, checking off what has been accomplished that week.

Though hardly a day goes by without Herr Schafer correcting me about something, when he sees that I am truly trying to learn, he promises me, "By the end of the summer, I'll have you laying bricks yourself."

I cannot tell him that any day I expect a letter, perhaps with train tickets, urging me to come to the Stauffenberg family. I imagine their pleasure in the reunion, how they will welcome me with open arms. I see myself strolling about on the grounds of their great home. Though I try to put it out of my mind, I can't help being a little angry with Mother and Father for not returning me to my rightful parents after the war.

Each day Mother places Father's mail on a little tray in his study. When he arrives home, after giving mother a kiss on the forehead, he goes to his study and examines his mail. Since we have the same name, Peter Liebig, I think that is where I will find my letter. I make an excuse to Father for not walking home with him. "I've got soccer practice with Kurt and Hans," I say. Then I take a shortcut to our house, quickly go over Father's letters, and leave before he gets there. Three days go by, and then I find the letter. It is the second one in the tray.

Dear Peter Liebig,

I am an attorney for the Stauffenberg family, who have asked me to reply to your letter.
Yours is not the first letter of its kind that the Stauffenberg family have received. I inform you as I informed the others that after the war's end, happily all the children of the Stauffenbergs were reunited with their family.

Yours very truly,
Karl Schneider
Attorney-at-Law

Will I ever find out who I am? I don't really belong to anyone. No one wants me. Well, maybe that's not true. I'm sure my parents love me, but what about my real parents? I know it could be worse, and I think of Gustav and what happened to his parents and how he is really alone. I guess I was counting too much on the letter. After I get over my disappointment, I tell myself that I am a snob because I daydreamed about being a part of a famous hero's aristocratic family. I turned my back on my own mother and father, although they have done everything for me, showing me love and affection every day. I feel guilty, but I am also miserable, because I still don't know who I am. If I'm not a Stauffenberg, who am I? What if I find out something I don't want to know?

EIGHT

I T'S HARD TO KEEP my mind on my work. When the bricks I piled up topple over into a heap, Herr Schafer says, "What's this sloppiness, Peter? You must have your mind on some girl." I feel my face grow red. I am glad to be busy. I work to the sound of Herr Brandt testing the organ, the deep tones of the music filling the church as if the music were water and the church a thirsty basin. Reiner Nordstrom is applying gold leaf to his decorations. The leaf is real gold and so thin that if you touch it, it flies apart, the bits of gold floating in the air. Herr Nordstrom applies it with a special brush and then burnishes it until it shines. The steeples reach a little farther into the air, landmarks now, because once again you can see them from a distance.

I hadn't planned to confess my worries to Herr Schafer, but we have grown close. Our lunches, taken together, always end in a discussion of something or other. It took a while before I saw that he launches these talks as a way of getting me to think. Whatever position I take, he takes the opposite. The Socratic method, he calls it. I know he was a philosopher, but our arguments are seldom about life-shaking issues.

"Which is more important in your sandwich, Peter, the liverwurst or the pickles?"

"The liverwurst."

"Would you eat the liverwurst without the pickles?"

"No way—the pickles hide the taste of the liverwurst. Mother says the liverwurst we get from the butcher shop is probably made from stray cats."

"Would you eat the pickles without the liverwurst?"

"Sure—I love pickles, especially the pickles Mother makes."

"If you would eat the pickles without the liverwurst, but not the liverwurst without the pickles, perhaps you need to rethink which is the more important of the two."

Then Herr Schafer has a good laugh.

Having found out there is a mystery about myself,

I begin to wonder if other people have secrets, so I ask him, "Weren't you a professor at Heidelberg University?"

"Yes, Peter. My days in Heidelberg were the happiest of my life, first as a student and then as a professor. Heidelberg is a student's dream. There is a romantic ruined castle standing on a hill. A peaceful river wanders through the town, and beside the river is the Philosophenweg, the philosophers' path, where great men like Goethe once wandered. There are cafés where students and professors talk and argue by the hour. To be a part of so great a university was all I wanted from life."

"But you couldn't have learned to lay bricks at the university," I said.

"No, Peter. That is not where I learned to lay bricks." He is quiet for a minute, as if he is deciding whether or not he can confide in me. He must decide he can, for he says, "The Nazis came along. They decreed Jews could not teach at universities. When I could no longer teach, it was misery to see my colleagues and students every day and know I could have nothing to do with them. Besides, I knew danger was coming and I wanted to be near my family. I went back to Hamburg, where I had grown up. My family lived in a pleasant flat near the Inner Alster, a pretty lake in the middle of town.

From the shores of the lake you could see the spires of five churches and the town hall. We were Reform Jews and went each sabbath to the synagogue, but we did not take our faith too seriously. We had many friends who were not Jewish. My father had been a successful lawyer. A year before, he had suffered a heart attack and had to retire. My mother was a curator at the fine arts museum. She had studied art in Paris and was an expert in her field of Chinese porcelain.

"Friends told my parents to leave Germany, but even after I had been expelled from the university, my parents said that leaving would be running away. Then it was decreed that if you were Jewish, you could not work at the museum, and Mother was separated forever from her beloved porcelains. At last my parents saw the danger ahead. By then it was too late to leave.

"One evening we were at dinner. My mother prided herself on her cooking. She was artistic in everything she did. It was my birthday, and she had baked a cake for me. She had been saving eggs and had some chocolate given to her by a friend at the museum who, in spite of the danger, remained close to my parents. With the precious ingredients so hard to get during the war, she had made my favorite chocolate cake, a *Schokoladentorte*. We all sat for a moment admiring it. Just as Mother raised the knife to cut the cake, the doorbell rang. We thought it might be a friend who lived nearby and by some magic had guessed Mother had made one of her famous cakes. Father started to get up, but to spare him, for he was quite weak then and every movement was an effort, I hurried to the door.

"Before I could get there, the door was battered down and six Gestapo officers rushed into the room. They had a paper with our names on it. "We give you five minutes to pack," they announced, as if they were doing us a great favor.

"Mother ran to Father, who was white as the table-cloth. He shook his head. "Never mind me. Go and get what we need, my dear. Take warm clothes and good shoes." So I knew he had been thinking this time might come. Mother and I ran upstairs. I helped her throw some clothes into a suitcase and I did the same. They were shouting at us to hurry, but Mother ran back to her room to snatch a picture of the three of us together taken on a picnic when I was still a boy and Father a healthy man.

"When we got downstairs, I saw that the torte had been eaten and the officers in their pristine uniforms and shiny boots had rings of chocolate around their mouths. To this day I cannot touch chocolate."

I can hardly bring myself to ask, but I have to. "What happened to your parents?"

"There were trucks outside. One for the young and healthy, and one for the sick and elderly. When I insisted on going with my parents, I was knocked down and shoved into the truck for the healthy. Later I learned that my parents were sent to Auschwitz, where they were killed almost at once.

"I was sent to a work camp, where they taught me how to make bricks. Like the Jews enslaved in Egypt, I made bricks for the enemy."

After a very long silence I ask, "Herr Schafer, why do you stay in Germany? You could go to another country and teach in its universities."

"Jews have lived in Germany for a thousand years, Peter. The Nazis took everything from me, but they could not take my country. It is not theirs to take."

"Why aren't you teaching here in Germany, then?"

"There aren't that many teaching positions. The universities are just getting back on their feet. Anyhow, I need to see the world a little more clearly before I go back to teaching students what they ought to think."

What I heard from Herr Schmidt were lectures. What I hear from Herr Schafer is real. "How can people be so evil?" I ask.

"There are some Jews, Peter, who believe that in every generation there are only thirty-six righteous people in the whole world and no one knows who they are. Without those thirty-six the world could not exist. For myself, I think there are many, many more. The difficulty, Peter, is that we often do not recognize evil. Evil can begin with a word."

Because Herr Schafer has been so frank with me, I believe I can talk with him about my worries. We are having our lunch on a bench in the shade of a tree. We look at the people moving about in the bright July afternoon as if we are watching a play on a lighted stage. In the distance someone is pushing a lawn mower, and I can smell the newly cut grass. In the trees, squirrels are hopping restlessly from branch to branch.

"Can I tell you a secret?" I ask.

"Of course, but keep in mind, Peter, that we tell secrets grudgingly—that is why they are secrets. If you tell me something you have been careful to keep to yourself, you may regret it and then you might become angry with me for hearing that secret. Think carefully before you tell a secret; and Peter, I must reserve the right to break my promise of secrecy if I feel it is for your welfare."

His solemn words nearly silence me, but I have

already determined that I will tell him. I open my mouth and the words tumble out. "It started because of Herr Schmidt at my school telling us about what happened to the Jewish people, people like you and your parents. My father was in the army and I got to worrying about what he did during the war, so I snooped around the house. I read letters Father had written to Mother." When I see Herr Schafer frown, I blush with embarrassment. "I shouldn't have, but I had to know." I blurt out the contents of the letters to him. "The really strange thing is that there is this picture of a woman and I recognize her." I tell him of my nightmares. "Father tells me I can't know the truth just yet. He promised to tell me who I am, but I'm not sure now I want to find out. I think maybe I'd just rather be me."

Herr Schafer is staring closely at me. "You believe that this woman might be your mother?"

"Yes, I believe she gave me to Mother. It's just like my nightmares—the woman giving me up."

Slowly, as if he isn't sure of how his words will come out, Herr Schafer says, "Peter, have you wondered why the woman had to leave her child and why your parents made such a secret of it?"

"At first I thought I might have been one of the children that they took away from Claus von Schauffenberg and his family. I even wrote to the family, but they got all their children back. Maybe my real mother was sick or poor."

"Poor people, even sick people, seldom give their children away, Peter. And wouldn't she have kept in touch with your mother; wouldn't she want to know what happened to you? I wonder that you haven't thought of people who were facing death for themselves and for their children as well."

Herr Shafer is looking at me in a strange way. It has never occurred to me that I might be Jewish. In my daydreams I have been the son of a hero like Stauffenberg, someone rich and maybe famous. I remember the crying woman and the look of misery on her face. Of course she could be Jewish. I have heard stories of Jewish children who were saved by someone taking them in and hiding them. St. Mary's Church stands only a short distance away. I look at the church. It is one thing for Herr Shafer to work there, but I belong there. I remember how Mother has wanted me to go to church and Father has never insisted. I can barely get the words out. "You think I might be Jewish?"

"Certainly it is a possibility. How would you feel about that?"

What would it be like to be Jewish? What would

Kurt and Hans say? There is St. Mary's, which I am so proud of. What if it's no longer my church? Once when I was little, I had been sailing a toy boat on the canal. The string attached to the boat broke. Before I could stretch out my hand to rescue it, the boat sailed away. Now, like that boat, my world is slipping away, the string that holds it together broken.

Herr Schafer must see the look of shock on my face, for at once he puts an arm around me. "*Ach*, Peter," he says. "I should never have suggested such a thing. It's my own sad experience that puts that thought into my head. I want to believe that someone has reached out to save a child as I wish someone had reached out to save my family. I'm sure there is a simple answer. Now it's time to get back to work."

Reluctantly I follow him back to St. Mary's and begin piling bricks on the pallet, thankful for the mindless work that leaves me to think my thoughts, which now are like tangled snakes I can't unravel, and am not even sure I want to. I like and admire Herr Schafer, but he is the only Jewish person I really know. Right after the war the city had no Jews; then a handful of Jewish families like his returned to the city. No one gives them trouble, but I have seen people stare at them and whisper after their passing. Complications pile up in my head faster than the bricks pile up on the pallet. Though he has tried to make little of his suggestion, I believe it at once. It all fits. There was Mother's letter to Father suggesting she had done something dangerous. There is Father's reluctance to make me go to church. There is Father's silence.

When the workday is over, Father is waiting for me. Reluctantly I walk along with him, hanging back so he will know I am angry and wish I weren't there. We walk in silence that is much louder than talk would be. When we reach the small park where Herr Schafer and I had our lunch, Father says, "Let's stop here a minute, Peter." The park is deserted. The kids who usually play there have gone home to supper, to homes where, when they walk through the door, they will be certain who their mothers and fathers are. This morning I saw the fledgling falcons teetering on the edge of their nest. Even the birds have homes.

Father puts his hand on my shoulder. "Peter, I am sorry that I put off giving you an answer, but I needed the time to think how I would tell your mother. These last days I have been wondering what to say to her. I know she doesn't want to talk about it, that she thinks it is better to put it behind us. But it isn't fair to you. Tonight I promise I will tell her."

Of course I know who Father means when he says "your mother." Now for the first time I realize my mother might be someone quite different. I ask myself, *Who is my mother and where is she?* It's not just a quiet question but a silent shout. I have to know at once.

"Father," I insist, "can't you at least tell me who my mother is?"

"Peter, if I could tell you I would. The truth is, I don't know."

NINE

I WALK INTO OUR HOUSE, but I don't. The boy who walks in isn't me. It wouldn't surprise me to find that the house and everything in it has vanished. The boy who isn't me looks around at all the familiar things, but they look as if they have come from some story that isn't real, right out of a book or a movie. In spite of what Father says about not knowing who my mother is or where she might be, I wonder if I shouldn't be there with her instead of here.

Father says, "Peter, please go upstairs and wash up for supper. I'll call when it's time to come down." The words come out sounding like Father is announcing the end of the world.

Mother has a puzzled expression and, underneath it, fear. "What is it, Bernhard? Why are you speaking in that tone of voice? Has something happened?"

Father shoots me a sharp look that sends me clambering up the stairway. I don't belong in my room, for the room belongs to the boy I was. My books, records, magazines, even my clothes have nothing to do with me. In all the familiar, I am a stranger. How can it be that they don't know where my real mother is? What does it mean for mothers to get lost? What if Mother and Father don't want to find my mother for fear she will take me away? What I can't decide is whether *I* want to find my real mother. What if I don't want to be her son? What if I have to move away from school and all my friends and from St. Mary's?

It doesn't seen fair to have to give up something just to have what was mine. Why should I have to choose between two lives, especially between a life that I know and a life I know nothing about? I want to stay right where I am, where everything is familiar. Yet the other life is something that belongs to me as well, something I have coming, something I must have. I know my mother and father love me, but what about the woman who is my *leibliche Mutter*, my birth mother—my *wirkliche Mutter*, my *real* mother? If she's alive, wouldn't she want her son with her? What if she needs me to take care of her? Maybe I can be with Mother and Father half the year and with her the other half—but then with two lives, I would be two boys. Wouldn't that be confusing? And if I turned out to be Jewish, what would that second life be like? And worst of all, Father has said he didn't know who my mother was. How is that possible? Where have I come from?

On my desk are my notes from Herr Schmidt's class. I remember how bored I was in that class and how I resented hearing about the fate of the Jews. That might have been my fate. I hear Mother, her voice always so low and calm, give a shrill cry. I head for the stairs and stop when I hear Mother say, "We agreed to silence on the matter."

Father says, "He has half guessed, Emma. He has a right to know."

"What is the good of bringing up the tragedy of that poor woman now? War is full of tragedies, but we can't go back and undo them all. We have to get on with our lives."

Father says something I can't hear. He's calling to me. Step by step I drag myself down the stairs, worried about what Mother will have to say to me. Will she be angry about my reading the letters? When I get downstairs, I see she is wiping away tears and I feel awful, as if all this is my fault.

"Peter," she says, "your father tells me you recognized the woman in the photo you saw, that she was the same woman who was in your nightmares, but that's impossible. You were only a toddler. Can't you put all that out of your head? It is only a nightmare."

"I have to know where my—my real mother is," I say. Immediately I am sorry, for who is more my real mother than the one who stands before me?

"*Real* mother? How can you ask such a question? I am your real mother. I have cared for you all these years. Who could love you more than I do?"

"We had better tell Peter everything," Father says. He takes a deep breath as though he is ready to run a long race, and then he plunges in, talking rapidly, getting it over with like a quick swallow of medicine. "When your mother and I were married, there was no thought of war. We only wanted to settle down and have a family. The bad days of the Depression were over. New buildings were going up in Germany. As an architect I was getting work. We had a pleasant home in Ulm with a bedroom for the child we hoped to have, but no child came along. We worried that we might never have a baby. Then the war came. I was drafted into the army as an architect; your mother and I were separated." He looks at Mother.

"I hated the war," Mother says, "but it was impossible to escape it. I gave up my teaching position and joined the Red Cross, where I thought at least I could do something to help those who were suffering. We met trainloads of wounded soldiers and tried to comfort them while they were awaiting medical care. It was heartbreaking, Peter. The trains and the wounded never stopped coming, the soldiers getting younger and the number of wounded increasing. Some of the returning soldiers told us stories of German losses that were never reported in the German papers."

I see Mother clench her hands. I feel terrible for her, but I must know. "Other trains came through the station while we were tending the soldiers. Those trains were boarded shut. They were like the trains that ship animals to a slaughterhouse. Sometimes we could hear pounding on the doors or the voices of people inside shouting. There were many guards with dogs around those trains, and at first we thought the cars were transporting Allied soldiers to prisoner-of-war camps. The German Red Cross distributed food packages sent from overseas to such soldiers, so I knew of those prisons.

"Rumors began to circulate about the sealed trains. The official story was that there were young men on the trains who were on their way to a work camp, but it was whispered that the trains held Jews forced to go to a concentration camp at Dachau. At first I refused to believe such stories; still, the pleadings and the screams from the trains haunted my dreams.

"There was no knowing when the trains with wounded soldiers would arrive in the station. The Allies had bombed the tracks all over Germany, and trains were often delayed, sometimes getting in late at night, so our Red Cross teams had to work around the clock. One night several trucks arrived at the station, pulling up just a few feet from me. Immediately soldiers with their guard dogs surrounded the trucks. When the doors were opened, hundreds of elderly people and women with little children spilled out and were herded by the soldiers toward a train that stood nearby. I saw at once the yellow stars sewn on the prisoners' clothes and knew they were Jews. We had heard rumors, but we didn't want to believe. Now the proof was right in front of me. There was a lot of confusion. The children were crying and some of them tried to run away. Peter, I wept. What had my country come to?"

As Mother talks, I think of Herr Schafer's parents. They would have been sent to their deaths on such trucks.

Mother sees the look on my face. "I am almost finished now, Peter. At that moment the attention of the soldiers was diverted to a truck where men were making an attempt to break loose. Some of the soldiers headed in that direction, leaving fewer to guard the truck near me. The prisoners passed by me in the dark, so close I could have reached out to touch them. When a woman holding a toddler in her arms bumped into me, I felt the warmth of the child against my chest and instinctively reached out my arms. 'Take him,' the woman begged. 'For the love of God, save him.'" Mother takes my hands in hers and holds them tightly. "Peter, how could I not do as she asked?

"There was only a second before the rest of the soldiers would return with their dogs and their guns. I was alone. The other Red Cross women were busy elsewhere. The remaining soldiers were occupied herding the people onto the train. No one was watching us. I tell you, Peter, to this day I don't know why I took you. Had I been caught, it would have meant prison or worse. I don't know whether it was my pity for your mother or my own wish to hold a child in my arms, or both. God will have to judge me, but I saved your life and that is what your mother wanted. You must never forget her sacrifice. To give you up must have been worse than death for her.

"I had a basket of sheets and bandages to use with the wounded soldiers. That is where I hid you, just as his mother hid baby Moses in a basket in the bulrushes."

I know the story from Sunday school. The pharaoh of Egypt ordered all the sons of the Jews killed. When a son was born to one Jewish woman, she took him and hid him by a river. The baby was found by the pharaoh's daughter, who saved the baby. The baby became Moses, who led the Jewish people out of Egypt to the promised land. I can't take in Mother's story, but one thing I understand. I say, "I'm Jewish."

"Peter," Mother said, "you are our son. That is the important thing."

"Father?" I look straight at him.

"Since your mother was surely Jewish, then you are Jewish, but the faith that you choose to follow will be up to you."

"What do you mean, Bernhard?" Mother asks. "Peter has been confirmed at St. Mary's. Surely he is a Christian."

There is only one question I want answered. "Where is my mother?"

Father shakes his head. "We have looked everywhere for her, Peter. Those trains went on to Dachau. We believe she was killed."

"But where did you get the picture?"

Mother says, "The picture was tucked into your jacket. We showed the picture to as many survivors as we could reach. No one could identify her."

"How do I know you really tried to find her? You say you always wanted a baby. What if you were afraid she would take me away from you?"

Mother begins to cry again. "Peter, how could you think such a thing? Do you believe we are so cold-hearted? It would kill me to give you up, but I would rather die than keep you from your mother."

Father says, "Peter, locked in my desk is a folder full of letters we sent. I will show them to you. Believe me, we tried. Did we hope she was alive? Of course. In our hearts she had become like a daughter to us. Did we want to keep you? Yes. But did we know you belonged with her? Yes, again. We only hoped that if we found her, she would allow us some part in your life."

Mother says, "All this is a shock for you, Peter. You must understand we did all we could. We have to put this behind us and get on with our lives." She stands up and, straightening out her apron, tries a smile, which doesn't work. She gives me a hug that nearly smothers me, and as she always does, she brushes back the hair that falls over my forehead. "Come—dinner is almost ready," she says. "I have made your favorite—spareribs and sauerkraut."

"If I'm Jewish, maybe I shouldn't eat pork."

Mother throws up her hands. "Peter, what are you saying? You are our son. That is all you need to know." She throws her arms around me, but I squeeze out of them.

It's too much for me. I run out of the house, slamming

the door behind me. I feel pulled apart, as if someone has one arm and someone else the other and they are both tugging at me. After the shock of hearing who I am—or really, who I am not—it dawns on me that only a miracle has kept me alive. If my mother hadn't given me up and my other mother hadn't taken me, I would have been killed like millions of other Jews. What Herr Schmidt taught in his class not only happened, but it happened to me! When I sat in his class bored and wishing I were somewhere else, somewhere I wouldn't have to listen to such terrible stories, how could I know I was listening to my own story?

All the while I walk, I ask myself questions. What does it mean that I was saved and millions of other Jews died? Was it just chance that the soldiers had their attention turned for a minute so that my birth mother could hold me out and my mother stretch out her arms for me? I can't get over the idea that maybe it is more than chance. Doesn't the Bible say a sparrow can't fall to the ground without God knowing it? So why did he save me and why did so many die? I have never thought about it like that. I had never asked questions; but now it is about me, and I have a lot of questions.

TEN

I THINK ABOUT THE BOY who wrote the letter to the Stauffenbergs. For a moment I wonder about how much of a hero Stauffenberg really was. When my own mother and the rest of the Jews were being rounded up, Stauffenberg was fighting to help Hitler win. Probably he wanted Germany to win. But he was German, so why wouldn't he? I don't feel the same about him now.

For the first time I think of my mother and father and how what they did was brave too. Herr Schmidt told us that it meant death for anyone to hide a Jew. My parents risked their lives just as Stauffenberg did. So weren't my parents heroes? That seems impossible—my father, with his glasses slipping down on his nose and his hair mussed from his habit of running his fingers through it when he's thinking; and Mother, with the carpet slippers she wears when her feet hurt from being on them all day at school, and the way she worries over whether her spätzle will be light enough and not too heavy with flour. Somehow I thought all heroes would be soldiers in the middle of a war. I never thought they could be just everyday people.

Then I think of my birth mother giving me up to save my life. She guessed what was going to happen to her. I imagine her holding on to me when I was little. How she would be careful not to let me wander away even for a minute, and yet she had the courage to put me into the arms of a stranger, knowing she would never see me again.

I can't find a way to keep all thoughts from jumbling up in my head. Over and over again I think of that night at the railway station. I see my birth mother dragged out of her home. Who was she? Did she lose herself in books the way I do? Did she make strudel like my mother? And who was my father? What did he do and what might I have done if I had followed in his footsteps? There is another whole life out there for me, like a shadow walking side by side with me. When I reach out for it, it disappears.

I have to talk with someone. I consider going to

Kurt's house or Hans's, but what will they think of me when they find out I'm Jewish? Will it make a difference? Maybe I shouldn't tell anyone, but I don't see how I can't talk about it; it's all I can think of. Without considering where I am going, I walk in the direction of St. Mary's. When I am a little way off, I look up at the two steeples that once again soar over the houses and watch over the town. I am proud of my part in the rebuilding of the church. Will that change? Maybe now that I know I am Jewish, I shouldn't have anything to do with St. Mary's, but I don't want to turn my back on the church. Herr Schafer is Jewish and he is proud of his work rebuilding St. Mary's.

As soon as I think of Herr Schafer, I know I must see him. He can explain to me all about being Jewish. He has told me where he lives, and I head there through a part of town that is new to me, so unfamiliar that it seems I am in another city altogether. He is renting two rooms in an old house in a street of ancient crumbling houses. Without considering what he might think of my suddenly appearing on his doorstep, I push the bell.

An elderly woman who looks like the witch in "Hansel and Gretel" lets me in. "Herr Schafer?" she asks. "The third floor. He's at home. I saw him only an hour ago mounting the stairs with a bag that I am sure held his dinner. I couldn't swear to it, but I believe I smelled pot roast. If you hurry up the stairway, you might find a bite or two left over for you." When she smiles, she no longer looks like a witch but only like a nice old woman you wouldn't mind having for a grandmother, one who is sure to bake you cookies.

I take the stairs two at a time, but when I reach Herr Schafer's door and raise my hand to knock, my hand won't move. I am just about to turn around and escape down the stairs when he opens the door.

"I thought I heard someone on the stairway," he says. "Come in, Peter. You're very welcome, but what brings you here? Is there a problem at St. Mary's?"

Herr Schafer leads me inside and motions me to sit down in a big chair. A blanket has been thrown over the chair. Where the blanket is pushed aside, I see holes in the upholstery with stuffing leaking out. The walls of the room are bare, but there are books crammed into a bookcase made from planks of wood and bricks and a small table and two chairs, one of which Herr Schafer now pulls out to sit on. I notice that he is wearing a sort of round circle of cloth on his head. On the table are the leftovers from his dinner. The landlady was right. It's pot roast.

Herr Schafer sees me staring at his plate. "Can I get you something to eat?"

I shake my head. The place in my stomach where my food usually goes is all closed up. I couldn't swallow a crumb. I can't wait another second to tell what has happened. I have so many thoughts in my head, I have to shake some of them out or I'll explode. What has happened this evening comes tumbling out. "So, I'm Jewish just like you, Herr Schafer. You have to tell me how to act."

His eyebrows go up. "How to act?"

"I wasn't brought up that way, so I don't know how to be Jewish." I look down at his plate. "Don't Jewish people have special food?"

"Peter, slow down. You've had a shock tonight. Let's take one thing at a time. Being Jewish has nothing to do with how you have been brought up."

Then he says just what Father said: "Your mother was surely Jewish; therefore Jews would consider you Jewish. If you choose to continue in the Christian faith, that is up to you. At any rate there is no blame over what you eat. There are many Jews who don't keep the dietary laws. I myself don't. There are as many ways of being a Jew as there are ways of being a Christian, and as many in my faith as in yours who are eager to criticize the choices you make.

"Judaism is a religion, a heritage, and a culture. For you, Peter, it is a heritage, certainly; it is not yet and may never be a religion; and as to a culture, an awareness, and a taking part in things Jewish, we will have to see. I must warn you things are not easy for a Jew even in today's Germany. Anti-Semitism is still strong in Germany. Chancellor Adenauer, the head of our Federal Republic of Germany, has chosen for his right-hand man a former Nazi official, one who took part in what happened to us Jews. Last year Adenauer went to Russia to demand that Nazi war criminals be released. The people of Berlin cheered Adenauer when he brought the criminals home.

"But Peter, if there are problems in being Jewish, there is also the honor of being one of those chosen by God for great things. Looking over your shoulder are the millions who came before you who have made something very fine from their Jewish heritage."

I can hardly take in his solemn words. None of that seems to have anything to do with me. What about me? All I care about is what I have learned about myself. "Herr Schafer, do you think my parents did all they could to find my real mother?"

"I know your father is a man to trust. If he told you

he tried to find your mother, then he tried. Even though you may never know her, the love that it took for your birth mother to give you up into the arms of a stranger should mean a great deal to you. When you are older and have a child of your own, it will mean even more. And Peter, consider the risk your mother took in taking you. She risked her life. Your parents were harboring a Jew when that was an offense that could have gotten them both a death sentence. Our Talmud says, 'When someone saves a life, it is as if that person had saved the whole world.'"

Of course that explains Father saying that he was proud of the chance he had once taken. I am that chance. "But what should I do now?" I ask.

"I think you need to talk with your parents about that and look into your heart, but surely you should learn something of your background." He notices me staring at his skullcap. He reaches into a drawer and brings out another black skullcap, which he hands to me. "It's an extra I have. It's a *kippah*, Peter, which you can keep. The kippah is worn to cover the head. *Kippah* means 'dome' in Hebrew. Sometimes it's called a yarmulke. Jews are aware that the Divine Presence is over us and we are in awe of that closeness. The Talmud says, 'Cover your head in order that the fear of heaven may be upon you.' It is worn especially when we are in a holy place like the synagogue, or we are praying or studying the Torah. I was wearing the kippah because I was eating and we consider our dining table as an altar before God. I do it in honor of my grandfather, whom I loved and who was an observant Jew and followed all the Orthodox rules. I myself am not an Orthodox Jew. So you see, Peter, there are many different ways to be Jewish, and sometimes it takes a lifetime to discover the one that is best for you."

In all the strangeness I try to find something familiar. "You and I believe in the same God, don't we, Herr Schafer?"

"Yes, yes, we worship the same God and we both have Abraham as the father of our faiths. The first five books of the Bible—Genesis, Exodus, Leviticus, Numbers, and Deuteronomy—are our Torah. We share the other books of the Old Testament as well, but many Jews believe the Torah has something extra. They believe that God had a long talk with Moses. He told Moses how to interpret his laws, everything from rules for marriage to rules for the care of animals. So they didn't have to guess how to behave in a certain situation—everything was covered. What a long talk they must have had, Peter, and what a memory Moses had to recall all that God revealed! When years later that conversation between God and Moses was finally set down in writing, it was called the Torah.

"Perhaps most important to you, Peter, Christians have their Jesus, while we are still waiting for our Messiah. But let us concentrate on what we have in common. I am a great lover of our German poets, but for me there is no poetry more beautiful than the Psalms. Christian and Jew alike share every one of those beautiful words. So you see there are many ways in which you and I are the same. And Peter, I know how much you love St. Mary's. You can love St. Mary's without being a Christian—I do.

"Now, Peter, that is enough for this evening. Your parents will wonder where you are. You must do nothing to make them unhappy. Remember, there is no need for a hasty decision. You are not an adult yet. Take your time, but let me help you to know something of your heritage."

I stuff my kippah into my pocket and go out into the street. Everything looks different to me. I know the trees are not Christian trees or Jewish trees and the buildings themselves are not Christian houses or Jewish houses, but things appear to take sides. The people who have planted the trees, the people in the houses are either Christian or Jewish, but Herr Schafer says to think of what we have in common.

A mutt runs along the sidewalk. He has the muzzle and coloring of a German shepherd, but he is small and his coat is long and shaggy like a collie's. Can your religion be a mix? Like the dog is? Probably not. There are no skullcaps at St. Mary's, and I guess they have no crosses in Herr Schafer's synagogue.

I walk alongside some rosebushes, and the smell of the blossoms is sweet. I think God had a great idea when he made roses; surely he didn't make them just for Christians or for Jews.

A dark-haired woman hurries out of one of the houses and quickly gets into a car that has pulled up. I only have a glimpse of her face. She is about the same age as my birth mother was in the picture, but of course my mother would be older now. Will I stare at every woman I see, wondering if she is my mother? Would I be disloyal to her to stay a Christian? If I become Jewish, what about Jesus? Can I abandon him? But wasn't he Jewish? My head is spinning.

Mother and Father are at the window watching for me. For a minute I think about making up some story about seeing Hans, but I am a poor liar. Besides, I don't see why I shouldn't talk with Herr Schafer. There are things he can tell me that they can't, things I have to know.

Father says, "Peter, let us handle this difficult situation in a mature manner. Nothing good can come from storming off. It is a time for calm and reason, not dramatics."

"Come and sit down, Peter," Mother says. "I've saved dinner for you."

I'm tired of my worries, and besides, I'm hungry. I sit down at the table, and tugging it out of my pocket, I put the skullcap on my head. "The table is an altar before God," I announce.

Mother looks as if I have struck her. Father is silent for a long enough time to make me really worried. Finally he says, "You've been to see Herr Schafer. I'm not surprised, but you need to listen a bit before you act. You must give yourself time. These matters have been discussed and argued for a thousand years and more. You want to make a decision at a snap of the fingers. You are too young to make such a decision."

"Herr Schafer said the same thing," I tell them, "but he says I should know something of my heritage."

Mother says, "Your heritage, Peter, is our heritage. You are our son. What could be more simple?"

Father puts his hand on Mother's arm. "We must be fair to the woman who gave Peter to us. We must think what she would have wanted."

"Surely she would have wanted Peter's happiness," Mother says. "Hasn't he been happy all these years? It's the bringing up of all these things that has made him unhappy."

We are all worn out. It's like rowing in the river against the current until you think you can't lift the oars one more time. We are all tired of the arguing and only want to go back to where we were before all this happened, but we don't know how. I don't know what else to do, so I pick up my fork and begin to eat. When I ask for a second helping, Mother smiles as she fills my plate and tells me to save room for the *Apfelstrudel* she has made for dessert.

I remember all the times I watched, fascinated, as Mother rolled out the pastry again and again until it covered the whole kitchen table and was so thin you could read through it. The sweet, crispy pastry melts in my mouth. Somehow the taste of the familiar dessert cheers and calms me.

After dinner Father leads me into the corner of the living room he uses as a study. When I was little, I liked to sit on the floor near the desk and spread out his big rolls of blueprint. I would study the plans and try to figure out what part of the church they pictured. I knew St. Mary's inside and out. It seemed a kind a miracle to me that you could go from the small drawings on the blueprints to the great church itself.

Father says, "It's strange, isn't it, that you should be getting lessons in your Jewish heritage from a friend you made at a Christian church."

"Herr Schafer is proud of what he does," I say. "I don't think he minds that it is a church."

"Did you know that on Sundays he works to repair a building he and some of his friends are using as a synagogue?"

"How do you know that?"

"Herr Schafer asked my advice on the plans." Father takes out a small roll of blueprint and spreads it out facing me on his desk. It shows a brick house only one story high. "Though there are only a dozen Jews in Rolfen, they are anxious to have a permanent home for their synagogue. At the moment they meet in one another's houses. So you see, Peter, while Herr Schafer is dedicated to his own place of worship, he is perfectly happy to help us with ours. The two faiths can live side by side, each helping the other without giving up its own beliefs. By all means learn what you wish from Herr Schafer, but you already have your faith."

"Why didn't you tell me the truth about my birth mother a long time ago?"

"I wanted to tell you the whole story, Peter, but your

mother was against it. She felt it would only upset and confuse you."

Maybe she was right, for I am upset and I am confused. "Wouldn't it have been better for me to know right from the beginning so I could get used to it from the time I was little?" I have another thought. "You moved away from Ulm," I point out. "Isn't that where my birth mother would have come to look for me?"

"The Jews in Bavaria were among the first victims of the Nazis. Even after the war there were still anti-Semitic groups near where we were living. It turned my stomach. I could not look at you, Peter, and put up with such poison. I couldn't bring you up in such an atmosphere."

Father takes out a pile of letters and files from his desk and hands them to me. "We tried everywhere to find your mother. The government has a bureau that helps in such things, and there are Jewish organizations also. All we know is that train was on the way to the Dachau concentration camp."

The answers to Father's inquiries used different words, but they all amounted to the same thing: *We regret we have no record that such a person existed.*

I want to shout at them that there is a proof that such a person existed, and it's me.

ELEVEN

I **CAN'T TAKE IT** all in. It's like being served a huge
pie. You know you can't eat it all, so you want someone else to share it with. The next day is Saturday and
I head for the marketplace in front of the *Rathaus*, the
town hall. I'm looking for Hans and Kurt. After our
little problem in Travemünde we decided to stay away
from there, and instead we settle for hanging around
the marketplace. Farmers have come from the country-
side bringing baskets of eggs, raspberries, gooseberries,
lettuces, cucumbers, tomatoes, and carrots. Cages hold
squawking chickens and geese. All the food is expensive, but because of the food shortages it disappears
almost at once. There are stalls where people sell their
handiwork: cleverly carved wooden wolves and bears,

marzipan candy, and handmade sweaters and rugs. There are East German refugees presiding over tables spread with the few belongings they were able to bring when they escaped, a sad display of bits of jewelry and quilts or a shabby overcoat they need to sell to buy food. I worry about what will keep them warm when winter comes.

I find Hans and Kurt, and the three of us hurry to the stall where they sell used books. We pool our money and buy a copy of a Western by Karl May, *Winnetou, the Apache Knight.* Karl May has written all these great books about the American West, and the amazing thing is he's never been there! You have to wonder how he can make it all seem real. Next we head for a stall where we get freshly baked sweet rolls. Frau Lantz greets us. "Well, gentlemen, what will it be this morning for your refined taste, *Nusskuchen* or perhaps a *Buchtel?*" Greedily we each select a *Buchtel,* with its pocket filled with jam, and go off to the steps of the *Rathaus* with our treats.

In as serious a voice as I can manage I say, "I've got something to tell you." They pay me no attention. Hans is busy stuffing his mouth with his *Buchtel,* the jam oozing out in a disgusting way. Kurt is counting his money to be sure he has been given the right change.

"I'm Jewish," I say.

They barely look at me. "Sure, and I'm Napoleon," Hans says.

"No, really. I mean it. I just found out."

"You can't be," Kurt says. "Your parents aren't. I see them in church every Sunday."

"But they aren't my parents."

Kurt gives me a disgusted look. "Sure, your parents are the king and queen of England."

Furious at not being taken seriously I blurt out the whole story, starting with the letters and ending with my discussion with Herr Schafer. At last I have their attention. Hans and Kurt are staring at me.

"You shouldn't go around blabbing about it," Kurt says.

"What do you mean blabbing? Apart from Herr Schafer, I only told you and Hans. Anyhow, why shouldn't I talk about it? It's the truth."

"Maybe it's the truth," Kurt said, "but you don't want people to know."

"Why not?"

"It could get you in trouble."

"What kind of trouble?"

Kurt looks embarrassed. "Well, I never mention that we come from East Germany, because there are a lot of people here who resent us, but they would never kill us. Think what they did to the Jews."

I feel a little scared. "That was under the Nazis."

Hans says, "Remember what Herr Schmidt says: There are still Nazis around."

I remember the couple at Travemünde and turn on Hans and Kurt. Angrily I say, "If you two would rather not be seen with me, just say so."

"Have you gone crazy?" Kurt exclaims. "That's not what we're saying. We're just saying that there are people around who still believe that awful stuff about Jews, so you ought to think twice about talking about it."

"Personally," Hans said, "I think it's kind of neat. Jews are sort of exotic. I mean, there's this Jewish man who lives near us and he has a long beard. He looks like something right out of the Bible, like God or something."

"Well, Herr Schafer looks perfectly normal. You'd never know he was Jewish." As soon as I say that, I wonder what's wrong with looking Jewish and if I look Jewish. So I ask.

Hans and Kurt study me for a long time, making me feel really embarrassed. Finally Hans announces, "You look pretty much like you looked before."

"What's that supposed to mean?"

"You know, normal."

"Well, then, if that's how I look, that's how Jews look. So it shouldn't make a difference."

Kurt says, "It'll still make a difference."

Hans suggests, "Why don't you try it out?"

"Try what out?"

"Your being Jewish."

"How am I supposed to try it out?"

Kurt says, "I'll pick a place. You and your father belong to the rowing club, don't you?"

"Sure."

"Well, they don't let just anyone join. They wouldn't let my father join because he's from East Germany and not from Rolfen. See if they let you be a member when they know you're Jewish."

"What am I supposed to do, march up to the boathouse and tell them I'm Jewish? Come on with me and I'll show you you're wrong." I want to believe what I say, but deep down I'm unsure. I remember a discussion our coach had with one of the sponsors of our rowing club about admitting a boy. "I don't know anything about his parents," the coach said. "You had better check on them." Now I wonder what he meant.

As usual the clubhouse is a mess of used towels, piled-up street shoes, and clothes. Our coach gives me an impatient look. "What do you want, Peter? Your team isn't scheduled until this afternoon, and you had better be in good form. You were lazy out there last week. Or did you come to meet your father? His team won't be back for another hour."

I remember how Herr Schafer always leaves work a little early on Fridays. Once he told me the Jewish sabbath is from sundown Friday to sundown Saturday. I say, "I was going to ask if I could change the day I race."

"What do you mean? You've been racing with that team all summer."

I feel Hans prod me. "Well, it's our sabbath until sundown, and I just think it would be better for me to do it another day, maybe after work some night."

"What do you mean, sabbath? What's gotten into you? Sunday is the day for church."

Suddenly I lose my nerve. "Yeah," I say, and walk away.

Hans and Kurt hurry after me. "Why didn't you tell him?" Hans asks.

"I'm not sure what my father would think," I say. "I should talk with him first."

"You were scared," Hans says.

"I wasn't and it's none of your business anyhow."

Kurt snaps, "So why did you tell us?"

"If you are going to make so much of it, I wish I hadn't."

After that we make our way in silence to Kurt's apartment. His father is working all day at the market, and Kurt's mother is out doing her weekly shopping, so we have the apartment to ourselves. We take turns reading aloud from *Winnetou.* The book is all about Jack Hildreth, a young American from out east who has gone west to survey a railroad. He learns to shoot and use the lasso and track buffalo and grizzly bears and is given the name Old Shatterhand. We stuff ourselves with *Schmierwurst*, a delicious sausage that Kurt's father brings home from the market. Afterward, our heads full of the book, we head for an overgrown part of the park that stands in for the Wild West. I am Old Shatterhand; Hans is Winnetou, an Apache chief's son; and Kurt is Kleki-Petrah, a German who has gone to the United States to become an Apache. We sneak behind trees and around bushes looking for Rattler and his gang, the enemy.

We toss around a lot of threats from the book. "My knife shall drink his blood!" I yell. Hans says, "This coyote pig dares insult me; my blade shall eat his bowels!" We hide in the bushes and capture one another. Finally we tie Hans/Winnetou to a tree, and then, crawling on our hands and knees, Kurt and I rescue him. People stare at us, but we don't care. We just give one of our bloodcurdling cries.

At the end of the book Shatterhand is adopted into the Apache tribe. He and Winnetou mingle a drop of blood each in a cup of Rio Pecos water and drink it. The chief says, "The souls of these two young men shall mingle until there is but one soul in them." I think how great it would be if being Jewish were as easy as being adopted into the Apache tribe.

All weekend my lack of courage at the rowing club gnaws at me, and on Monday while Herr Schafer and I are having lunch, I confess to him what happened.

"Peter, there's no need to go around informing people you're Jewish. Did you go around announcing you were a Christian? Why confront people? As long as you know what you are, that's what's important."

"But I don't know."

"Being Jewish is not a game like checkers with a set of rules. Any Jew, or any Christian for that matter, will tell you we find out a little more about ourselves every day. What we were yesterday we are not today and will not be tomorrow. Don't be in such a hurry, Peter. Let each day teach you something, even if it comes from a mistake. Sometimes mistakes are the biggest lessons of all. How would you like to lay a course of bricks yourself? We have left the entrance to the courtyard for last so that the large trucks could go through without damaging the bricks. Now we'll finish the job."

For weeks I have been waiting for this chance. I long to be able to be a part of rebuilding St. Mary's. I want to walk casually by the church and say to someone, "Oh, by the way, you see that row of bricks? Well, that's my handiwork." I will show it to my children and they will show it to their children. I can barely hold the trowel. I am sure I will make a mess of it.

"Take your time, Peter. Remember, the bricks you lay will support all the rows that come after. While you are doing my work for me, I'll just mix a new batch of mortar."

I know Herr Schafer is leaving me on my own so I won't be nervous about having him look over my shoulder, but what if I make a mistake and he isn't there to get me out of trouble? He has told me a thousand times that a building is only as strong as its foundation. I throw a mortar line along the last course of bricks, putting on enough to hold the bricks but not so much that the mortar will get all over the other bricks when I smooth it off. I think of my mother frosting cakes. Mother once said to me, "You have to have enough icing, Peter, so that when you spread it the cake crumbs don't show through." When we go to church on Sunday, I'll show Mother what I have done. I think how pleased she will be. I lay the bricks, tapping them in lightly and then scraping away the excess mortar.

Soon Herr Schafer is back examining my work. I hold my breath. "Excellent, Peter," he says. "We'll make a mason out of you yet. Now, since it's Friday, I'm off a little early as usual."

"What do you do on your sabbath?"

"On Sabbath, or what we call Shabbat, I have a special Shabbat dinner with friends of mine."

"How do you mean, special?"

"I'll tell you what. I'll speak to my friends and get them to invite you to have dinner with us next week. First I want to ask your father's permission."

TWELVE

HERR SCHAFER DOESN'T FORGET the invitation. Later that week I hear Mother and Father having a long whispered conversation in the kitchen, after which Mother, looking very upset, and Father, looking sheepish, summon me. Father says, "Peter, Herr Schafer has kindly invited you to a Shabbat dinner with him Friday evening, and we've agreed that you may go."

"You'll be on your best behavior, Peter," Mother says. "It's very kind of Herr Schafer's friends to include you."

Mother's words surprise me. Somehow I expected that she would have forbidden me to go, but what she says next surprises me even more.

"I've been thinking this last week, Peter, of your

mother. I'm becoming accustomed to calling her your mother, for that's what she surely is. She and I are together in that. It would not be fair to her to let you grow up ignorant of the faith of your grandparents and great-grandparents and who knows how many generations before them. Only remember, Peter, you're our son as well, for we've been your parents every minute and every hour all these years. I'll not say that we love you more than your mother, but I'll not say we love you less."

Mother's words stay with me as I wait for Herr Schafer to take me to the Shabbat dinner. I have no idea what to expect—something different, I'm sure. Will the food be strange and will I be able to eat it? I think of the Jewish people roaming around in the desert eating that weird manna God sent them that tasted like wafers made with honey, so something like that would be all right. When he comes for me, Herr Schafer wears a dark suit and felt hat. I hardly recognize him out of his overalls and cap. He looks to me more like the professor he once was. Father greets him formally, shaking his hand and introducing him to Mother, who also shakes his hand. When all the hand shaking is finished, Herr Schafer says, "It is very kind of you to allow Peter to share in our Shabbat dinner."

Mother mumbles something, and Father says, "Peter has been looking forward to the evening."

Looking forward is not quite the proper phrase; *worried* or even *terrified* would be closer to the truth. I meekly follow Herr Schafer, glad Mother has had me wear my good church suit. We walk down the Mengstrasse with its fine homes and, turning a corner, arrive in a neighborhood of small houses crowded together as if they were hanging on to one another for company. Herr Schafer leads me to one of the smallest. The door is opened by a man and woman even before we push the bell, and standing next to them is Ruth Kassel. I can't help blushing, remembering how she caught me staring at her in Herr Schmidt's class.

"Please meet Herr and Frau Kassel, Peter, and their daughter, Ruth. Lisa, Leon, Ruth, this is my young friend, Peter."

Immediately the Kassels have their arms around me, welcoming me and drawing me into their home while Ruth stands there, grinning at my surprise. All this time, seeing her in school every day, I had no idea she was Jewish. Herr Kassel says, "We've been looking forward to meeting you, Peter. Herr Schafer has said such interesting things about you. Come in, come in."

I'm amazed that someone has interesting things

to say about me and wonder what they can be. The Kassels shepherd me into a small sitting room as if I were some long-lost son they've been waiting for. The room is small, but the furnishings are large, as if a regular-size sofa and chairs have been wedged into a dollhouse. I squeeze myself between a table and the sofa and settle onto a chair. Herr Kassel has an intense, worried look, as if someone has given him an impossible problem to solve and only five minutes to do it. Frau Kassel is more easygoing and not at all flustered to have a strange boy turn up in her home. She pats a cushion on the sofa, a friendly invitation to me to sit next to her. Ruth sits across from us. Instead of the skirt and blouse she wears at school, she has on a dress made of silk, and her long hair, still damp on the ends, is neatly brushed back.

Frau Kassel smiles at me. "Ruth tells me you are in her class and that you are a good student and very polite."

"Mother," Ruth says, "I didn't say 'polite.'"

The mother gives me a little pat. "Well, we can see that for ourselves."

Herr Kassel says, "Mama has prepared a fine Shabbat dinner for you, Peter. Herr Schafer tells me this will be your first."

"Yes, sir," I say. "I didn't know about my being

Jewish until a little while ago."

Herr Kassel peers at me through his wire-framed glasses. "That must have come as a surprise to you, Peter."

"Yes, sir. At first I couldn't take it all in, but now I sort of feel like I got a Christmas present I didn't expect."

At that Ruth giggles.

"Yes, yes," Herr Kassel says. "A Christmas present, eh?"

I blush. Of course the Kassels wouldn't be giving one another Christmas presents. How stupid can I be? "I should have said birthday present."

Frau Kassel says, "A present is a pleasant thing, never mind when you receive it. Now, dinner is ready."

We move into a dining room only large enough for a table and five chairs. Frau Kassel lights some candles and Herr Kassel pours out some grape juice into little glasses that he passes around. Then Ruth says something in a language I can't understand but I guess is a kind of grace. Ruth recites it just as she does the poetry we are assigned to memorize in school, every word very clear, letting you know she has done her lesson. Then Ruth and the Kassels drink their grape juice, so I drink mine too. Herr Kassel lifts two loaves of bread high and says something else in what sounds like the same language, then sprinkles the bread with salt and gives us each a piece to eat.

There is no manna. Frau Kassel has cooked a tasty dinner of chicken, potato pancakes, and an *Apfelkuchen*.

Ruth sits next to me, and while the Kassels and Herr Schafer are talking about the building of their synagogue, she says, "It must be strange not knowing who your mother is."

"Yes. I've been thinking about her a lot. I keep hoping she didn't die, and I look at women in the street thinking I might just bump into her." This is the first time I have admitted that to anyone, but Ruth has been looking at me with her large brown eyes and I feel I could tell her anything.

"My grandparents disappeared," Ruth says. "I keep hoping that one day they'll just walk into our house like you did tonight and surprise us. My parents got out just in time—otherwise they would have ended up in a concentration camp like my grandparents did."

"I didn't know you were Jewish," I say.

"I didn't know you were either," she says, and gives me one of her grins. I imagine what it will be like to return to school in the fall with Ruth and if we'll give each other knowing looks like we share a secret.

When dinner is over, Ruth takes me to her room,

which is a tiny cubbyhole just large enough for a bed and dresser. On the walls are Ruth's paintings. I have seen Ruth's work in art class. Like most of the girls, she paints pictures of gardens with flowers and the seashore with the sun shining on the water and sailboats riding on the waves, so I am shocked at what I see here. The paintings are of rabbits or squirrels or puppies running around in the grass under some trees, and that's okay, but overhead in the branches of the trees are huge black birds with bald bloodred heads and great yellow beaks ready to pounce on the little animals. I get shivers. She sees my frown.

"Mother says she wishes I would paint something pretty to cheer her up and Papa won't come into my room, but I don't care. I paint what I'm supposed to in class, but in my own room I can paint what I want, only don't tell anyone in school."

I promise I won't. I tell her, "There's nothing to worry about. That happened a long time ago." She doesn't look convinced, and something tells me her mother and father have already said the same thing to her. I don't know why she is painting such gloomy pictures that are like a warning. I'm anxious to leave the sad room and get back to the Kassels' living room, where there is laughter and conversation and everyone is alive.

Soon it's time to go. I thank the Kassels and receive a warm handshake from Herr Kassel, a hug from Frau Kassel, and a shy smile from Ruth, who hangs back as if she is already sorry she showed me her paintings. When I shake hands with her, I give her soft hand a squeeze to let her know she can trust me not to say anything at school.

There is a light drizzle and the buildings and streets are shiny under the streetlamps. As Herr Schafer and I pass the houses, I look into the lighted windows. Every house, I decide, has its own secrets.

THIRTEEN

THE NEXT NIGHT Hans and Kurt are at the door after dinner, Hans looking like there is someone chasing him with a knife, Kurt casting suspicious looks over his shoulder. "We have to talk to you right away," Kurt says.

"Right away," Hans echoes.

"You don't have to whisper," I say. "My mother and father are at their friends' house playing pinochle."

They follow me into the sitting room and perch warily on the edge of the sofa as if someone might pull it out from under them. "You're in danger," Kurt says.

"What do you mean?" I look around to see if someone is hiding behind one of the chairs.

Kurt nudges Hans. "You tell him."

Hans takes a long breath and looks important. "I was carrying up some packages for a man who was checking into the hotel. They weren't wrapped very well and one of them came open. It was full of leaflets, hundreds of them."

"What kind of a leaflet, and what's that got to do with me?"

"You're Jewish, aren't you?" Hans says. "The leaflet said terrible things about Jews and how Germany was right to get rid of them and how they oughtn't to be allowed to come back. The man arranged to have a meeting tomorrow night at the hotel. He's distributing these leaflets to get people to come." Hans pulls a wrinkled piece of paper from his pocket and hands it to me, holding it by the edge as if it might catch fire and burn him.

I read the leaflet. People of Rolfen are warned that more and more Jews are making their home here. They are building a synagogue. Soon, it says, the Jews will own the banks and take over the businesses. The leaflet instructs people to act before it's too late and to refuse to rent or sell houses to Jews or to do business with them. It's illustrated with ugly pictures of Jews. At first I feel fear, but soon the fear changes into anger and I'm furious. I think of Ruth's paintings. What would it do to her if she were to see such a message? She would say she was right to paint such frightening pictures. I tear the leaflet in half, but what good does that do? There are hundreds more of them.

Hans says, "Maybe you ought to leave town, and you should tell your Jewish boss at the church."

"*Bist du verrückt*? Are you crazy? Besides, Herr Schafer would never be scared into leaving town and I don't intend to leave either." Somehow in spite of the couple I overheard in Travemünde, I hadn't believed Herr Schmidt and Herr Schafer when they told me that there were still people in Germany who hated Jews. Now that I had to believe them, what was I going to do? Hans and Kurt are looking at me, waiting to see. "I'm going to break up their meeting," I say.

Kurt says, "You could get into trouble with the police," but Hans jumps up and slaps me on the back.

"I'll help you. I know the hotel backward and forward. We can figure out something." I can see his mind racing. Knowing Hans, I suspect it isn't so much a matter of stopping the meeting as the thrill of having some fun. "The meeting is at nine in the evening," he says. "If we wait for a half hour or so, it will be dark."

"So what? There are lights inside the room," Kurt says.

Hans looks important. "I know where the fuse box is. All I would have to do is pull a lever and I could make the room dark in a second."

"They'll just light candles," Kurt says. He isn't convinced.

Hans says, "First they'll have to find the candles, and I can see to it that they're well hidden."

I'm trying to think of something I read not long before in the Rolfen newspaper. Suddenly it comes to me. The article was about a new sprinkler system the hotel had placed in all the rooms in case of a fire. It's the first sprinkler system to be installed in Rolfen, so the paper made a lot of it, saying the town is becoming up-to-date. I turn to Hans. "Do you know how the sprinkler system works?"

"Sure. Heat sets it off."

I'm figuring things out as I go. "So if you hold a cigarette lighter up near the sensor, it will trigger the sprinklers?"

Hans catches on. "If you hold it up close enough, it will set the system off and everyone in the room will get soaked. Where will you get the lighter?"

"My father gave up smoking last New Year's, so he never uses his cigarette lighter. He keeps it in his desk. You take care of the fuse box," I say. "I'll take care of the lighter." We clasp hands.

Kurt looks unhappy. "What am I supposed to do?" All at once a look of inspiration lights his face. "Leave the rest to me," he says.

Together Hans and I demand, "What are you planning?" Kurt only shakes his head. "You'll find out tomorrow night."

"We're going to have to figure out everything to the minute," I say. "It'll have to be like an army invasion with split-second timing. Hans turns off the lights right at nine thirty. As soon as they go off, I hold the lighter up to the sprinkler system. But how am I going to get into the hotel, and how will I reach the sprinkler system? It must be up by the ceiling."

"I'll put a stepladder right next to the window. The windows are close to the ground and they're always left open in the summer for meetings because the room gets hot and stinky from cigars. They won't pay any attention to the ladder because they're still doing a lot of repairs to the hotel. The minute the lights go out, you come in the window and climb up the ladder. I'll put white tape on the rungs so you can see them. Use the lighter, and as soon as the sprinklers go off, climb out the window and take off."

By the time Mother and Father get home, we have

everything planned. Seeing us sitting huddled together, Mother asks, "What are the three of you up to? You all look like you got caught with your hands in the cookie jar."

Hans gives Mom one of his goofy smiles. "We were just figuring out if we have enough money to go to the movie tomorrow night. It's an American film about the war with Burt Lancaster."

"The war!" Mother makes a face. "Why would you want to see a film about the war? All that is over with."

Father pats Mother on the shoulder. "It's only a movie, Emma. Let them have their night out; they've all been working hard this summer. They can't get into mischief in a movie theater." He pulls out some deutschmarks from his wallet and hands them to me. "The movie's on me."

The three of us head for the soccer field, eager to run off some of the excitement we feel. On the way we stop at the hotel kitchen to collect Gustav, who we have learned is a good soccer player. He whips off his apron and hurries away with us. "I've been working since five this morning. We've got a special dinner tomorrow night and I made *Kaisersemmeln*. They're Viennese dinner rolls you have to fold in a special way. You make a little ball and then you pull out some wings from the little ball and fold them into the center with a special twist, like this—" Gustav does a little dance with his thumb and two fingers.

He wants to go into more detail about the *Kaisersemmeln*, but Hans interrupts him. "Hey, let's go before it gets dark." We don't say anything to Gustav about our plans for the meeting. We could probably trust Gustav, but maybe he'd worry that his precious *Kaisersemmeln* would get all wet.

There are only the four of us, so Hans and Kurt stand together on an imaginary line, with Gustav and me across the field from them. They're the defenders and we're the attackers. They kick the ball to us and we try to get the ball over the line. Kurt stays back. Hans starts toward us. He's looking for an opening to get the ball from us. After a while we switch partners and sides because Gustav is taller than we are and all over the field.

When it's too dark to play anymore, we lay our sweaty bodies down on the cool evening grass and look up at the stars. It's August and the time of year when you see falling stars.

Gustav says he's dating Greta, who works as a cook's helper at the hotel. "One day the two of us might open our own restaurant. Just a little place but everything fresh and tasty."

I never give much thought to what I will do. I don't want to spend my life laying bricks. Maybe I'll be an architect like my father. I wish I knew what my birth father did. That would be something to consider as well.

Hans tells us he is taking Hilda Moser to the movies.

"She's older than you," Kurt says.

"Yeah, so I'll learn something from her."

I wonder if Ruth would go to the movies with me. I decide if she smiles at me when school starts, I'll ask her.

Suddenly Hans shouts, "There, over there, a falling star." Sure enough a star is hurtling down the dark sky.

Kurt says, "That's not a star. That's a meteoroid, little bits of rock and dust that fall into the earth's atmosphere and burn up."

The three of us jump on Kurt. "Say it's a star," we insist, pinning him down; but when we let him up he says, "Meteoroid."

Twice the next day Herr Schafer has to get after me for not piling up the bricks properly. "What are you thinking about, Peter?" he asks. "Keep your mind on your work." I want to confide in him, but something tells me that he wouldn't approve.

Since I have already talked about going to the movies, there are no questions asked the next evening when I leave the house. Father calls out, "Have a good time."

Hans is already across the street from the hotel waiting for me. A minute later Kurt arrives struggling with a big box. The box is moving in his arms and making strange sounds. "What's in there?" Hans demands.

Kurt looks pleased with himself. "A pig."

I can't believe what I hear. "A pig! Where did you get a pig, and what are you doing with it here?"

"It's only a little one. A farmer came into the butcher shop a couple of days ago with some pigs, and he had a litter of piglets in his truck. I begged Pa for one as a pet. He said I could have it until school starts and then it gets butchered."

"I'm really happy that you can have a pig to play with," I say, "but why is it here? We don't have time to admire your new pet."

Kurt waits a minute until he has our full attention. "I greased it real good with lard. After Peter climbs out of the window, the pig goes in. When it has had a little time to run around, Hans will turn the lights on and catch it."

Hans and I look at each other and begin laughing. I clap Kurt on the shoulder. "You're a genius."

Kurt doesn't deny it. "You'll be sure and get my pig back?" he says, looking a little worried.

Hans promises, "Believe me, my one goal in life will be to get my arms around your pig."

Across the street men, singly and in pairs, are beginning to go into the hotel. They look over their shoulders and shoot quick glances at one another. I thought the men would be ugly and threatening looking. Instead they look like everyone else. I recognize a man who has a tobacco shop where Father sometimes stops for a newspaper. I've often been there with Father, and the man has given me chewing gum. I begin to get cold feet. It's one thing to break up a meeting of evil men, but these men look perfectly normal. Then I think about what the leaflets say and I get angry all over again.

"I've got to go," Hans says. "The ladder is just inside the window. Have you got the lighter?"

I pat my pocket.

"Did you check to be sure it has fluid?"

"I'm not stupid," I say. "I wasn't planning to rub two sticks together. It's all set to go."

There's no need to check my watch. The clock on the town hall is so close, it seems to look over our shoulders. When we hear it chime the quarter hour, we make our way to the window at the back of the hotel. No one is in sight. The front of the hotel is neatly landscaped, but the alley at the back is a jumble of old lumber and trash cans that stink of rotten potatoes and decaying vegetables. The kitchen must be nearby, because I can smell onions cooking. The smell makes my stomach turn over. When a rat scurries over my shoe, I have to slap my hand over my mouth to keep from crying out. Just as Hans promises, the window is open. In fact two windows are open. I haven't planned on that. Which window is the right one? I look at Kurt.

"It must be the one that's open all the way. You'd have trouble getting through the other one." Crouched under the window, we can hear voices coming from the room, loud voices. "I tell you we have to act now!" someone is saying. "Why should we wait for a change in the government? By then the Jews will be in charge of all our businesses."

The clock chimes the half hour. The lights go out. I can't move. My feet are frozen to the ground. "Go ahead," Kurt whispers, and gives me a little push. He bends over so I can climb on his back. The next thing I know, I'm dropping into the room. It's pitch dark and men are moving around shouting complaints. Some of them are fumbling with their own cigarette lighters. We hadn't counted on that. What if they see me before I can trigger the sprinklers? I feel for the ladder, and before I lose my nerve I scramble up the highlighted rungs. The first flick of the lighter doesn't trigger a flame. I try again. The second time the flame flares up, illuminating the sprinkler pipes. I hold the lighter close to one of the sprinkler heads. For a moment nothing happens. I hear someone say, "What's that light on the ceiling?"

Suddenly I feel a spray of water. The next minute I'm out in the alley. Kurt pushes me aside and holds up his box to the window. I hear a thud and then a loud squeal as the pig lands. There are cries of surprise and anger coming from all over the room as water gushes out of the pipes. Cries become shouts of "Catch it!" There are thuds of bodies crashing to the floor. A minute later the lights go on. We peek in the window. It's chaos. Men are sitting or lying down, their suits soaked, their glasses at the ends of their noses, their hair plastered down with water. A couple of men are chasing the pig, but it slips out of their grasp. Suddenly right in the middle of everything there is Hans assuring the men he will catch the pig, which is trotting back and forth, squealing with terror.

Hans drops a tablecloth over the pig and scoops it up. Someone says, "That's right. Get that fool animal out of here." Hans hurries off with his armful of pig. A minute later he joins us, and the three of us hurry from the hotel as fast as we can, laughing so hard we can barely run.

With the pig safely in its box, we huddle together behind some houses waiting for my hair and shirt to dry in the warm summer night while keeping an eye on the movie to see when it's over. We keep telling one another what happened. "They were falling down like bowling pins," Hans said.

"That was my pig," Kurt boasts.

"I just walked in and scooped it up," Hans says, "and one of the men gave me three deutschmarks."

"I should get half," Kurt said. "You couldn't have caught the pig if I hadn't put it there."

Hans says, "I've got some money saved. I'll add it to that and buy a new size-five soccer ball and we can all use it." Kurt, who loves soccer as much as he loves telling people what to do, is satisfied.

The doors of the movie theater open and people began to stream out. I give my wet hair a final pat and button Hans's sweater over my damp shirt. We shake hands and solemnly promise never to reveal what we have done; then we all head in different directions, the sound of Hans whistling following me for the first block.

Mother and Father are sitting on the steps of the front porch having their nighttime cups of tea. "Well, how was the movie?" Father asks.

"It was great. Lots of excitement."

"Not nearly as much excitement as there was at the hotel tonight."

"What do you mean?" I ask.

"Well," Mother says, "Herr Heintz next door was at the bar of the hotel having a beer and there was some sort of meeting in the next room. Suddenly all the lights went out. A minute later the sprinkler system was triggered. According to Heintz the men at the meeting were up to no good. Anyhow, they all got soaked, and what's more, a greased pig got loose in their midst."

Father says, "Whatever those men were up to, I don't think they'll be having any more meetings here in Rolfen. Too bad you were at the movies and missed all the fun."

FOURTEEN

I LONG TO TELL Herr Schafer about our adventure, but I don't want to get Hans or Kurt into trouble. I have pledged silence and I won't break my word. Herr Schafer arrives at work with his dinner as well as his lunch pail. "Why are you bringing your dinner with you?" I ask.

"Some friends and I are turning an old building into a synagogue, and we want to finish the work before the cold weather comes. I lay bricks all day and then I do the same until dark." He laughs. "At night I dream about laying bricks."

"Dad showed me the plans for your synagogue. Maybe I could help you." I'm curious about what a synagogue looks like. Besides, Herr Schafer works on our church, so I don't see why I can't work on his synagogue.

"By all means come and help, but only if it's agreeable to your parents and only for an occasional evening. Your vacation is coming to an end, and you won't want to spend the few evenings you have left laying bricks."

After supper that evening I slip out of the house, saying nothing to my parents, for I could see my going to the dinner with the Kassels worried them. Every time I get ready to leave the house, they ask me in roundabout ways what I'm going to do and who I'm going to be with. I'm not going to lie to my parents, but I don't want to cause them any more worry, so on this night I sneak out while they're listening to the evening news on the radio.

I have no trouble finding the little house Herr Schafer and his friends are turning into a synagogue. One tumbledown wall and half of a second wall have been repaired. Herr Schafer and Herr Kassel welcome me, but the third man, a Herr Schocken, only nods in a brusk way and, glowering at me, goes on with his carpentry work.

Herr Schafer explains, "We have more than ten Jewish men now in Rolfen, which means that we can have our own house of prayer. Several gather here every day and a few men come twice a day." Church twice a day! I am suddenly less enthusiastic about the Jewish religion. Herr Schafer sees the look on my face, and laughing, he says, "I'm afraid I'm not so observant. I come only once a week and on holidays."

He takes me inside to show me the building, which surprises me, because the inside is nearly finished. "We're working from the inside out so we can have services. Christians have an altar, Peter; we have the Holy Ark, which contains the Torah." Sheltering the ark is a velvet curtain. Herr Schafer says it was sewn by Mrs. Kassel. "This stand is like a pulpit. It's where we read the Torah." There is a lantern with a little light in it. "The eternal light," he explains, "to remind us of the lamp in the Temple in Jerusalem, which never went out."

After showing me around, he says, "Now I must get back to my bricks. I see you have come in your work clothes, so if you want to help, you are welcome."

When we join the others, Herr Schafer surprises me by saying, "Peter is skilled enough to lay bricks with me; he's been doing that at St. Mary's."

At that Herr Schocken does some more glowering and grumbles, "David, this is no playground for boys to learn a trade. Let him learn at St. Mary's. If he wants to do something, he can put the bricks where you can get at them."

Herr Schafer has his mouth open to say something, but he closes it again and nods in the direction of the pile of bricks that stands on the sidewalk. In no time I am watering bricks down and piling them up, and Herr Schocken, noticing I'm working hard, is no longer glowering. I stick it out for two hours. Herr Schafer and the other men are still working when I leave. It's warm out and I feel hot and sweaty from my work. My back aches and there is a scrape on my hand that burns. A huge August moon climbs up from the horizon, making a gold path on the canal. I remember that Hans and Kurt have talked about going for a swim. I wish I had gone with them. I'm still angry at Herr Schocken for not letting me help to lay the bricks. I decide he can build his synagogue without me.

Hans is as good as his word and has bought a new soccer ball. In the days before school starts, the three of us spend all our extra time practicing, hoping to make the team when school opens. The last evenings of summer cannot be long enough. I gulp down my supper and am out the door to meet Kurt and Hans on the field we have appropriated for our practice. The evenings are a little cooler now, the dark comes quicker, the hours seem shorter. Hans is a wild man on the soccer field, everywhere at once, taking risks and making huge misses and terrific kicks. Kurt is careful and accurate. He doesn't always get the ball, but when he does, he knows what to do with it. I'm halfway between. What I love about the game is that the only thing I need to think about is what's going on on the field. When it's too dark to see the ball, we walk slowly home, not wanting the night to end, knowing each day brings us closer to school.

No one is happier with my nightly soccer practice than my mother and father. Once when I slip back into the house to change my shoes, I overhear Mother say, "We have our Peter back again." I know they hope I have put the question of my birth mother out of my head. Of course I haven't. I am just trying to keep so busy, I won't have time to think about her or about anything connected with that other life. I can't keep busy every minute, so there are still times when I wonder what my life would be if there had been no war and no death camps, if I and my birth mother and father had lived out our lives together. I try to guess what my home would have been like. Perhaps I would have had brothers and sisters and aunts and uncles and cousins. It makes me sad to think that that life will never be except in my imagination.

Herr Schafer and I still have our lunches together, but he doesn't mention my Jewish heritage. I know he is waiting for me to be the first to mention it. I avoid the subject. Our talk now is of the celebration that is coming for the completion of St. Mary's. When the last bricks are laid, Herr Schafer says good-bye to me. We promise to keep in touch. When I ask how the synagogue is coming along, feeling a little guilty about not having returned to help, he says it will soon be finished.

The Sunday we celebrate St. Mary's completion, the whole town turns out in their best clothes. It is an early-fall day and the sky is a deep blue. Once more the bells ring out across the town. The church is so filled with flowers, it looks as if spring has come again. At the organ Herr Brandt plays a fine tune that I am sure must be something by his favorite composer, Bach. The deep chords of the organ fill the church and make me feel I have been picked up and shaken. The sun shines on the gilded wood and lights fires in the blues and reds of the stained-glass windows. The choristers in their new robes, black as night and white as snow, march down the aisle to Luther's hymn "A Mighty Fortress Is Our God," and indeed, St. Mary's seems like the fortress of a great lord. Pastor Heuer, his glasses shining in the candlelight, mounts the pulpit and opens the ancient Bible that has been a part of the church for hundreds of years. Above us the steeples reach high into heaven and the service begins. Mother clasps my hand. Father heaves a deep sigh as if he has just put down a great burden. I see tears in his eyes.

To keep the workmen from getting too conceited about their work, Pastor Heuer clears his throat and reads from the Old Testament, " 'For every house is builded by some man; but he that built all things is God.' "

After the service people come up to Father and congratulate him on his part in restoring the church. There is a special dinner at the town hall for all the workmen. Herr Schafer isn't at the service, but he is there at the dinner. I am caught in the crush around Father, and by the time I break away, Herr Schafer is gone. I resolve to visit him before the week is over, but all week there are the tryouts for the school soccer team. When Hans, Kurt, and I make the team, after-school hours are taken up with practice. Being on the team gives me a higher status at school. I never lack for lunch partners, and Ruth Kassel agrees to go to the movies with me. My assignment on Stauffenberg got me a good mark from Herr Schmidt, but that all seems a long time ago. My nightmares have disappeared. I look at my parents in a new way. I think of the chance they took for me. If it weren't for their courage, I wouldn't be here, going to school, walking down the streets of Rolfen on a fine September day. Every step I take is a gift from them—and from my birth mother.

It's a day in late October. Many of the trees are bare, and Mother has taken in all her flowerpots because of a threat of an early-morning frost. In a good mood because our soccer coach has made me a forward, I'm helping Mother dry the dinner dishes, taking pleasure in holding the glasses up to the light to be sure all the smudges are gone. Father is sitting at the kitchen table turning over the pages of the newspaper, mumbling to himself as he does when there's some political nonsense that excites him. Suddenly he lets out a little gasp, as if someone has punched him in the stomach.

"Bernhard, what is it?" Mother asks.

Father opens his mouth and then shuts it as if he can't make up his mind about telling us. I bend over his shoulder and see a small article headlined NEW ROLFEN SYNAGOGUE SET ON FIRE. I take in the rest of the article at a gulp, throw down the dish towel, grab my jacket, and am out the door, ignoring Father's plea to wait. The article says the fire occurred on the day before the synagogue was to celebrate its opening. I'm sure someone has watched the efforts of Herr Schafer and the others, cruelly waiting until they were finished.

The wooden door to the synagogue and the roof are badly burned. Herr Schafer, Herr Schocken, and Herr Kassel are on the roof tearing off scorched shingles. A group of silent watchers, mostly kids, stands about. I walk up to them and say in an angry voice, "If you aren't going to help, you can take off instead of standing there gawking!" Embarrassed, they melt away.

I gather up the discarded shingles and stack them neatly and then at Herr Schafer's bidding open a bundle of new shingles that lies beside the building and carry them up a ladder to give to the men. Herr Schocken hands me an extra hammer. "Herr Schafer will show you how," he says. There is no grumbling and no talk of my learning at their expense. We work steadily with little conversation, only a few sly jokes between Herr Kassel and Herr Schafer about who is working faster versus who is making a better job of it.

When it becomes too dark to see what we are doing, we climb down from the roof. Herr Kassel and Herr Schocken go on their way. Herr Schafer says, "We're all taking turns sleeping here to keep watch. Tonight it's my turn. It's good of you to help, Peter. I can't think why there must be this destruction of the places where people go to find their God. It's like the wood carving in St. Mary's of the little mouse gnawing at the roots of an oak tree. It takes only a few evil people to eat away at the character of a town. Every unkind act cheapens this town and makes it easier for the next person to commit some spitefulness.

"But Peter, some good has come of the evil. Many people on this street have brought us food while we worked, and like yourself, they have lent us a hand. Still it was a cruel thing, and between you and me, Peter, it made me think of leaving Rolfen. Last week I had a letter inviting me to come to a university in the United States. I miss teaching and I feel my life is wasted in the laying of bricks. I was ready to accept, but now I don't know. It would be running away from my friends at a difficult time. Germany is still my *Vaterland*, my homeland, and I won't turn it over to a few hoodlums."

"Do you know who did it, Herr Schafer?"

"The firemen knew it was arson. They could tell almost at once what started the fire from the smell. It was carbon tetrachloride, a chemical used in dry-cleaning shops."

Dieter Kroner's name pops into my head. "There's this boy at school whose father owns a dry-cleaning store. He never believed what Herr Schmidt told us in class about what happened to Jews. I'll bet he did it."

"The fire department and the police are investigating.

Leave it to them, Peter. I'm not interested in revenge. Revenge begets revenge. Let's not speak of it anymore. Tell me how you are. I've missed our talks."

"I wanted to see you, but I made the soccer team and there's practice in the afternoons and then at night some of us get together for a scrimmage." The minute the words are out of my mouth, I realize what a lame excuse it is.

"Peter, you'd never believe it from the belly I carry around now, but when I was your age I was quite the soccer player. I played at Heidelberg University. Maybe I'll come and watch one of your practices."

I walk home from the synagogue in darkness. Pads of damp leaves lie long the sidewalk and smell of autumn. It's the strong smell of the leaves that makes me think of Herr Schafer saying the firemen could smell carbon tetrachloride. I don't want to believe that Dieter would have done something so evil, and even if he had, I wouldn't know how to prove it. Without proof it would be wrong to accuse him. I don't understand how God could let such things happen. Father always says, "Don't judge God by what men do," but life seems very mysterious, full of questions and not a lot of answers.

I ask myself why I have made no move to practice my Jewish faith. Do I sincerely believe the Christian faith in which I was raised, or am I just avoiding a lot of the kind of hatred that caused the burning of the synagogue? When I see ahead of me the lighted windows of our house, I start to run as if someone is chasing me and our house is the only safe place in the world.

To my surprise Herr Schafer turns up the next night for our soccer scrimmage. Anyone interested can play. Herr Buchhalter, the chemistry teacher from school, is there most nights. Karl Mann, a policeman, comes with his red-and-blue striped shirt, and Gustav Uhlich comes too. Werner Kreutzer, the barber, is umpire. Kreutzer actually saw the World Cup championship game when Germany won in 1954, so having him here makes our scrimmage seem like the real thing. Everyone knows Kreutzer longs to play, but he weighs about three hundred pounds and even blowing his whistle leaves him short of breath.

Kurt, Gustav, Hans, and I are on the same team, while Gerhart Miller and Dieter Kroner usually play on the other team. On this night they have seven on their team, while we have to play with just six since our seventh player has come down with measles and there isn't time to get a substitute.

Herr Schafer stands watching the play, his legs moving a little like he wants to get in the action. Gerhart and

Dieter give him a funny look. I kick the ball in his direction. He stops the ball with his chest, and the next thing I know he's in the game and all over the field, juggling like there is no ground under his feet. With Herr Schafer on our side, we get the ball down to the goal and he gets it past the goalkeeper with a slider.

Dieter is furious. He glares at Herr Schafer. "We don't want to play with Jews!" he shouts.

Herr Kreutzer trots out and shoves a yellow card at Dieter. "Watch your language, sonny," he says, "or you'll be out of the game." Kreutzer, with a big grin on his face, turns to Herr Schafer. "I guess you've played this game once or twice before."

Herr Schafer doesn't hog the ball. He keeps passing it, but when it comes his way he's phenomenal, running right into the ball and making it go where he wants it. Our team catches fire and scores two goals.

"Hey, we're all going to be Jews tonight!" Hans shouts at Dieter. "And we'll beat the stuffing out of your team!"

I watch Dieter shadowing Herr Schafer, and on the next play he works his way next to him and lets go with a high kick, his foot only inches from Herr Schafer's head. Kreutzer goes puffing out with a red card and Dieter is out of the game, left to stand on the sidelines digging trenches in the ground with his cleats.

Even though Herr Schafer sees to it that everyone on our team gets a chance at the ball, that can't prevent our winning by a wide margin. While both teams crowd around him, I walk over to Dieter, who's standing there with his hands tightened into fists.

"Your dad missing any of his carbon tetrachloride? Maybe you needed a little for a chemistry experiment? Maybe we should ask the police to help you find it?"

Dieter looks as if someone just pushed him into a wall face-first. That tells me all I need to know. At first I want to lunge at him, but what Dieter has done is bigger than anything I can punish him for.

I tell Herr Schafer. He says again he doesn't want revenge, but adds, "Justice is something else." He tells me he has received a letter from a friend at his old university in Heidelberg. "It isn't exactly a job offer," he says, "but someone there knows I'm still here."

I head home, passing St. Mary's. It soars over the town and I think of all it has seen and how it has survived. Some of St. Mary's bricks have been here for nearly a thousand years. I run my hand along the course of bricks I laid. If there are no more wars, no more people hurting one another, my bricks might be here for the next seven hundred years. Father is already working on plans to rebuild a smaller church across the city. He will go on bringing churches back to life and I will go on listening to Herr Schafer's stories, and someday the two will come together and tell me what to do.

It's Friday and school is over for the week. Ruth wasn't in school today because it's the first day of Rosh Hashanah, which is the Jewish New Year. I think I would like to do something to celebrate the day. I walk along nibbling a *Buchtel* I've saved from my lunch. As I cross the river Tave that circles the city, I remember Herr Schafer telling me about the Tashlich service. On the first day of Rosh Hashanah crumbs are cast into a river where there are fish. The crumbs represent our sins for the year, and the river carries them away. The fish are important because fish were the first witnesses to creation. Because their eyes are always open, they are like God's ever-watching eyes. I toss some of the *Buchtel* crumbs into the water and feel lighter, as if a lot of my worries have been thrown away with the crumbs. Then I eat the rest, licking the jam off my lips, thinking of all that is sweet in my life.